ATALAN ADVENTURES

by

Richard Brewin

Chapter 1

The car came to a stop on the driveway outside the picturesque little cottage, the gravel crunching underneath the wheels of the white family saloon signalling its arrival. The car looked like it had just completed an off-road rally stage, its bright white paintwork now a mucky shade of brown. It may have been the middle of summer, but like so often with the Great British weather, there had been plenty of rainfall causing the country lanes, which had to be navigated to reach this destination, to become a slalom of puddles.

The car belonged to the James family. Jackie and Peter sat in the front, and their daughter Isla was in the back gazing out of the window looking exceptionally bored. Isla turned to watch her dad wrestle with the handbrake.

This was something that seemed to happen every time they finished a journey. The ritual was always the same: Dad struggling to lift the handbrake, while Mum told him, "You should really get that looked at," and his response always the same, "It's just a bit stiff, that's all," before Mum would have the last word by saying, "One of these days the car will roll away."

Isla smiled to herself. She often imagined coming out the family home one day and finding that the car had vanished after Dad had lost the battle with the brake and it had simply rolled away down the hill.

She could hear her mum now telling Dad, "I told you so," and giving him one of those looks that only mums can give!

Once Dad was happy that he was safely parked and there was no danger of it rolling away and ending up in a neighbour's bush, he climbed out of the car and threw his arms out wide and arched his back to stretch his weary body. He let out a noise that sounded somewhat of a combination of a yawn and a sigh. The noise made Isla chuckle as she fiddled with her seatbelt. Mum opened the passenger door and beckoned Isla out; she grabbed her backpack and shuffled out into the heat of the summer afternoon. The rain had stopped, and the sun was now beating down, causing a rainbow to form in the sky over the cottage.

The cottage belonged to Isla's Grandma Mary and, as the wooden sign that hung on the wall by the front door proudly announced, it was named Willow cottage, mainly due to the large weeping willow tree that stood in the middle of the immaculately kept front garden.

Isla loved this tree and had spent many hours in the past sat underneath it writing stories and drawing pictures as the branches cascaded down like a floral umbrella all around her. It would be the perfect place for a game of hide and seek, Isla had often thought to herself; it was a shame she didn't have anyone to be the seeker.

Every summer in the school holidays, Isla would spend a few days here while her parents had to work. It wasn't as if she hated coming to Willow cottage and spending time with her grandma, it just wasn't the most exciting of places for a 10-year-old girl. She would much rather be at home hanging out with her friends or, if not doing that, at least sat in her bedroom texting and facetiming them or snapchatting them selfies complete with bunny ears, halos, and giant licking tongues. If she wasn't talking to her friends, she would be making and playing with slime or watching children on YouTube making and playing with slime, which was a pastime that seemed to baffle her parents.

Unfortunately, there would be no such slime activities at Grandma's as it was banned ever since the great slime explosion last Christmas. Turkey and slime certainly wasn't a Christmas delicacy that anyone wanted to taste again in a hurry. As well as the lack of slime, there also would be no communicating with her friends as you could never get a signal at Willow cottage, and Grandma didn't have Wi-Fi or, according to Isla, had probably never even heard of the internet. In fact, there wasn't even a television set here; the last one had stopped working a few years ago and had never been replaced.

Isla had often asked her grandma why she didn't have a T.V, and her dad had offered to buy her a new one on numerous occasions, but she always declined.

She would remark, "What's the point in having something I don't use. I make my own entertainment, thank you very much." By own entertainment she meant sitting in her favourite chair knitting countless hats, scarfs, or jumpers, reading one of her many books, or tending to the garden. Even though Grandma's cottage was only a couple of hours drive away from the James family home, because of this distinct lack of modern technology, to a 10-year-old girl it felt like the middle of nowhere.

Dad gave three loud knocks using the ornate golden lion's head knocker that proudly hung in the centre of the old wooden front door. On either side of the door hung two hanging baskets overflowing with brightly coloured flowers which created a welcoming aroma. The James family stood in silence, waiting for the door to be unlocked. Dad jangled his loose change in his pockets; Mum admired the baskets and sniffed the flowers as if they were expensive bottles of perfume; Isla stood at the back looking down at her white trainers intently as if they were the most amazing things she had ever seen.

Dad was about to knock again when there was the sound of keys rattling from the other side

6

followed by the noise of bolts being pulled back before the door opened with an eerie creek.

Mary stood in the doorway with a welcoming smile. She was small in stature, not much taller than Isla. Her white hair was tightly curled and was almost the colour of the cardigan she was wearing which was fastened all the way up with little buttons that resembled pearls that glistened and sparkled every time the sunlight hit them. Her skirt was long and chequered, and on her feet, she wore cream booty style slippers that had been hand-knitted. The usual greetings were exchanged, hugs for her son and daughter-in-law and a big sloppy kiss on her granddaughter's forehead.

"Come in, come in, and close the door behind you," said Grandma as she disappeared into the cottage. "You must be tired after the journey; cups of tea for everyone?" asking the question to no one in particular as she walked through the small hallway and into the lounge which led onto the kitchen situated at the back of the cottage.

The hallway wasn't very big at all with just enough room for Mum, Dad, and Isla and their bags to all fit. In it was a small narrow table that stood about waist height that had an old fashioned telephone perched on it or at least it was old fashioned to Isla! Anything that had to be plugged in and wasn't touchscreen was old fashioned to a ten-year-old.

Above the table hung a pendulum wall clock that made a faint tick-tock sound. The Roman numerals on its face told the James family that it was half past twelve. The door to the lounge was directly opposite the front door, and a passageway ran off to the left of the hall. This led to a bathroom, two bedrooms and a back room which looked out over the rear garden and was where Grandma liked to sit and do her knitting.

As Grandma made her way through to the kitchen to put the kettle on, a parping sound seemed to follow her, possibly from the floorboards, Isla thought, as the cottage was very old. After the third such sound, a smell wafted its way into the hallway; as soon as it hit Isla's nostrils she knew what it was immediately….cabbage!

"We haven't interrupted your dinner have we, Mum?" shouted Dad, noticing the time.

"Oh no dear, I've just had some cabbage soup," came the reply.

Dad turned to Isla and flashed her a smile and a wink as she tried to stifle a chuckle. Grandma was well-known for making such noises and smells, thanks largely to her love of cabbage. Whether it was in a soup or a pie or being served up in her favourite cabbage surprise, the only real surprise was what else if anything had she used in it. Cabbage was usually on the menu at Grandma's house. Add the fact that her hearing wasn't as good as it used to be, which meant she would often walk

8

around the house parping as she went without even realising.

"There goes Grandma playing her bum trumpet," said Dad with a chuckle, a term he affectionately used for these occurrences and one that always made Isla laugh out loud. Mum, on the other hand, just looked at her husband and rolled her eyes at the fact he still found breaking wind so amusing for a man in his forties.

"Will you take your bags to your room for me, Isla, and put your clothes in the wardrobe, please?" asked Mum as she handed her daughter the black sports bag she had been carrying that contained her clothes and toiletries.

Isla took it in her left hand and threw her backpack over her right shoulder. It contained the important stuff needed for the stay, such as her dolls, drawing books, and pens. Once loaded up, she moved off down the short hallway towards the spare bedroom, which was hers for the next few days. She passed the bathroom on her right before coming to her room; from here the passageway went round the corner to the right and led to the main bedroom and the back room which had access to the rear garden via a pair of French doors.

As Isla pushed open the bedroom door, it welcomed her with the same eerie creek as the front door had. She walked into the small but neatly kept room and threw the sports bag onto the floor before carefully placing her backpack onto the floral duvet that covered the single bed.

She reached into the back pocket of her jeans and pulled out her phone and gave it a quick signal check; as expected, it read no service. She placed it back into her back pocket and went about emptying her bag.

Her backpack had seen better days, but she loved it, and it went everywhere with her. On the front was a large printed picture of a German Shepherd. Isla was a huge animal lover, especially dogs, and the German Shepherd was by far her favourite breed. She would have loved a dog, but so far her parents were not succumbing to her pleas. Out of the bag, she pulled three small dolls along with an old takeaway container which had accessories and clothes for them all neatly packed inside.

Along with these, there were a couple of colouring books, a drawing pad, a notebook, and a brown fluffy pencil case with a face at one end that resembled a dog. At the very bottom of the bag, hidden away, was a small tub of slime that she had managed to sneak in.

Isla picked up the books and pencil case and took them over to an old fashioned writing desk that stood at the end of the bed against the wall. It had a small wooden stool underneath which Isla pulled out and sat down; as she did, it gave out an unnerving creek, and for a second, Isla had visions of it collapsing and ending up in a heap on the floor.

Isla would often spend hours sat here colouring or writing stories. She had a wonderful imagination and would put pen to paper and create amazing adventures about fairies and elves who lived in a far off land.

She opened up her notebook and turned to an empty page before taking her favourite pen from the pencil case. Her grandma had bought it for her last birthday, and, like many things of Isla's, it was decorated in a doggy design. It had also been badly chewed at the end, which was something she did to most of her pens much to her Mum's annoyance. She was always telling Isla to "take that out of your mouth." Isla placed the end of the pen into her mouth and stared out the window which was above the desk and looked out onto the front of the cottage. She could see from here that Dad's car hadn't rolled away.

The sun was still shining brightly, and at this time of day, it shone directly onto the front of the cottage and into the spare room. So much so, the glare from it was making it difficult for Isla to see what she was doing. She leant forward from the stool and closed the flowery curtains which matched the bed covers before returning to her seat. She took the pen from her mouth and started writing. Before long, she had filled a page of her book; stories seemed to come easy for her.

Today's adventure was about a family of elves who lived under Grandma's willow tree and the mischief they got into, sneaking into the cottage at night and moving things around and generally creating havoc. She was three pages into her story when she heard her mum calling from the lounge that she and Dad would be leaving shortly so to come and say goodbye. As she put her pen down and got up carefully from the rickety stool, she heard her mum shout again.

"Have you put your clothes away neatly in the wardrobe?"

Isla picked up the sports bag that she had discarded on the floor and opened the small wooden wardrobe that stood next to the desk in the corner of the room. She threw the bag inside and shut the door. It may not quite have been what Mum had meant by "neatly," but it would do for now.

With that done, Isla made her way back towards the lounge. Mum and Dad were in the hall saying their goodbyes to Grandma. Isla gave them both a hug and a kiss, and Dad ruffled her hair.

"Be good for Grandma, and we will call you each night on the home phone."

"We love you and will miss you," Mum added as she opened the front door.

Isla stood in the doorway and watched her parents climb into the car. Grandma came and joined her and put her arm around her as the car's engine murmured into life. They watched Dad

12

wrestle once again with the handbrake, this time opting for the two-handed yank technique to release it before the car reversed slowly off the drive and disappeared to the sounds of a beeping horn and a chorus of goodbyes shouted through the windows. Isla waved until the car had vanished completely out of view before heading back inside.

"Come and sit down, my dear, and I will make you a drink," said Grandma as she shepherded Isla through to the lounge.

Isla slumped down onto the maroon leather sofa and watched Grandma disappear into the kitchen. The lounge was fairly small but was packed full of objects, ornaments, and pictures.

Isla's granddad, who had sadly passed away just over five years ago, had spent many a weekend wandering around antique fairs looking for hidden gems and collectable objects, and many of these had ended up on display in the lounge.

Opposite the sofa, there was an ornate fireplace with a real coal fire sat in the middle. Grandma no longer used the fire, but on the fireplace, there were all the tools needed to make one, from a coal bucket to shovels and a poker and each one in polished brass. On the shelf above the fireplace was a row of twenty or more model houses creating its own miniature town.

There was a church, pub, village shop and a garage just to name a few. Lying on the floor in front of the fire was a large white rug that Isla loved to lie on at night while reading a book before she went to bed. It was so fluffy and warm, and she often found herself nodding off on it as it was so comfy.

Next to the rug was a wooden coffee table that was made to look like an old fashioned cart complete with large metal wheels on both sides and two smaller ones at either end that reminded Isla of shopping trolley wheels. Apparently, the table was actually made from a reclaimed cart once used in an old local cotton mill. Isla knew this as it had been one of Granddad's favourite possessions, and Grandma had told her on numerous occasions all about the history of this particular piece of furniture. On top of the table were a couple of flowery patterned coasters and a large cardboard box that was overflowing with stuff. Isla leant forward from the sofa to get a better look at the contents of the box as Grandma returned from the kitchen with her drink.

"That's a box of stuff that I've had donated for the bric-a-brac stall I'm running at the church's summer fair," said Grandma as she placed Isla's glass of orange juice down onto one of the coasters.

Isla didn't really know what bric-a-brac was, but by what she could see sticking out of the box, it meant other people's rubbish that had been given to Grandma rather than being thrown into the bin.

Sticking out the top of the box were a couple of books that had seen better days: both had torn front covers and seemed to be held together by tape. There was a jigsaw puzzle of what looked to be a pencil case that had been emptied out all over a table, a label on the box lid read "one piece missing." Resting on top of the jigsaw was a Rubik's cube that had one of its coloured squares peeled off and then coloured back in with what looked like felt tip pen.

"I was sorting through this box before you arrived to see what treasures I could find. I should really move it into the back room with the other boxes. I don't think your granddad would have appreciated a box of junk on his mill cart, do you, Isla?" asked Grandma with a smile.

Isla gave her a smile back and shook her head in agreement.

"I've seen a few toys in the other boxes if you want to have a look through them. I think there might have even been some dolls. If you find anything that you like, you're more than welcome to them. I don't think the church would mind."

Isla's ears pricked up at the mention of dolls.

"Ok, Grandma, I will go and take a look." She was up and out the sofa before she had even finished the sentence.

"Don't forget your drink," said Grandma.

Isla picked up the glass and downed the orange juice in one gulp.

"Thanks, Grandma," said Isla as she wiped her mouth with her hand before disappearing out of the living room.

As Isla walked into the back room, she spotted two large boxes straight away, both of them filled to the brim with all sorts of rubbish. One of the boxes had "bric-a-brac" scribbled on the side in black marker pen, while the other box had obviously been used for a different purpose in the past. The words "Christmas decorations" were scrawled all over it. Either that or someone had very strange ideas about what Christmas decorations were, thought Isla. Apart from the boxes, there wasn't much else in the room.

Before Granddad had died, he had used it for what he had called his reading room, and there was still an old wooden bookcase in the corner that was full of his books. Both her grandparents had loved sitting in here reading and looking at the view out the French doors, and it wasn't hard to see why. At the bottom of the immaculately kept lawn, which looked like it had been cut with scissors, was a low fence. Behind this was a small brook.

Over the brook were lush green fields as far as the eye could see. Dotted along the edge of the fields were beautiful elm trees, and on one of these trees, hanging from a sturdy branch, was a rope swing that Isla had put up last year with a little help from her dad. All she had to do was hop over the fence and jump the narrow brook and then she could swing away to her heart's content while Grandma sat in her favourite spot knitting and keeping an eye on her.

Grandma's favourite spot was the comfy looking armchair complete with footstool that was positioned in the centre of the room facing the doors. A pair of knitting needles and a big ball of blue wool rested on the arm, ready for Grandma to start her next creation.

Isla knelt down and started rummaging through the first box marked bric-a-brac. The first thing she came to was an old fashioned looking gold plated lamp that resembled something you would expect to find a genie in. She instinctively gave it a rub, but the only thing that happened was a cloud of dust went up her nose and made her cough and splutter. She placed the genieless lamp on the floor and continued her search.

She found an English dictionary, a couple of mugs celebrating a royal wedding, a cuckoo clock that seemed to be working even though it appeared the cuckoo had flown away, and a figurine of a woman holding an umbrella who, unfortunately, had lost an arm.

After carefully moving the figurine to one side so she didn't lose any more limbs, Isla spotted what she had been looking for. Sticking up from the bottom of the box was a pair of doll's legs. She reached down and lifted them out, relieved to see they were still attached to a body. The only slight issue was this doll that was dressed as a beautiful fairy princess now had a head of an action man stuck on it, complete with moving eyes and a scar across his right cheek.

She looked back inside the box and saw another pair of legs sticking up that were dressed in camo trousers. When she pulled this one out the box, she discovered a burley soldier dressed in battle fatigues complete with flowing blonde locks and a princess crown on its head. Isla wondered just what sort of game the owner of these dolls had been playing as she placed them back in the box a little bit disappointed at her finds.

Once the first box had been repacked of its items, she moved on to the Christmas decorations box. She removed a couple of plates off the top that were wrapped in paper and came across an old looking leather bound book.

Normally, she wouldn't have given something like this a second glance, but this was different. On the front, the words "Atalan Adventures" were written in gold in an old fashioned font. She had no idea what or who "Atalan" was, but it wasn't the title that had drawn her to the book. Underneath the title was a picture of what looked like to Isla as to be two small elves. They were both dressed in dark green tunics with a red collar and stripy green trousers, complete with a red and green hat.

The most interesting thing about the book though, was the fact it had a shiny gold lock on it to stop you from opening it. The only time Isla had seen a book like this was last Christmas when her parents had bought her a secret diary that had a padlock on it to keep prying eyes out. Of course, once Isla spotted the lock on the book, she immediately wanted to do what any curious ten-year-old would want to do and that was to open it; all she had to do first was find the key.

She emptied the second box in search of the missing key removing such things as a box of playing cards, a couple of pictures, a copper teapot with a dint in it, a game of Scrabble that appeared to be missing tiles, and a small statue of a Buddha.

Just as she was about to give up the search, she spotted something glistening at the bottom of the box. She reached down and picked up the small but very ornately decorated golden key. The handle of the key appeared to have the head of some kind of creature on it; to Isla, it resembled that of a goblin.

She carefully placed the key into the book's lock and turned. She heard a faint click, and the book fell open in her hands. The page it opened on had a large picture on it depicting a forest. It was so clear and lifelike, the bright green colours of the trees almost jumping out of the page. As she studied the picture closely, it was almost like the leaves were blowing in the wind and as if you could hear them rustling. She lifted the book up closer to her face and stared intently and almost dropped it in shock.

The leaves were really blowing in the wind! It must be one of those magic eye pictures, Isla thought, where you look at it for so long and another picture appears, or maybe some kind of hologram. But the more she looked at it, the more the leaves started to blow, and the sound of the wind whistling through the forest got louder and louder. It was almost like she could reach out and touch the trees and pull the leaves off a branch, maybe she really could.

Holding the book in her left hand, she slowly moved her right one towards the picture. As her fingers reached the page, they kept on going, her hand literally disappearing inside the book. She let out a cry of amazement as the book engulfed her entire arm, and then her whole body was pulled through the page…WOOOSSHHH. Suddenly she was falling and falling fast!

Chapter 2

Everything around her was white. She tried to scream but no sound came out. All of a sudden, it was if she had passed through a tunnel and the whiteness was replaced by many different shades of green. She was falling through a forest and the floor was approaching fast. Isla closed her eyes tightly and braced herself for impact, but before she hit the ground, her fall was broken by something or someone.

Isla lay still for a second trying to get her bearings and figure out exactly where she was when underneath her came a muffled scream.

"Hey, what do you think you're doing? Get off me!" The voice made Isla jump up. Luckily, nothing appeared to be broken as she sprang to her feet. Apart from being slightly shaken, she was perfectly ok.

"I'm ever so sorry," Isla replied to the small boy who was lying prone on the floor beneath her in a pile of leaves.

"Hey, you can't just go jumping out of trees like that and not look who is below you," came an angry voice from behind her.

Isla turned around to see another small boy standing behind her. He was a fair bit shorter than Isla, although facially he looked slightly older. He was wearing a green tunic with a red collar along

21

with green and red stripy trousers. On his head, he wore a green hat complete with red trim that matched his red face.

"I'm so sorry," Isla exclaimed. "I didn't jump out of a tree; in fact, I don't know how I ended up here, where even is here?" she asked, looking around at the forest that she was currently stood in.

Wherever here was it was certainly beautiful: trees as far as the eye could see all covered in different shades of vibrant green leaves. Rays of sunlight beat down through the tree canopy, and a slight wind rustled through the forest.

"You don't know where you are?!" said the boy who she hadn't landed on top of. He scratched his mop of blonde hair that was poking out from underneath his hat, looking a little confused.

"This is Atalan," he almost shouted, pointing all around the forest as he said it.

Geography wasn't Isla's strongest subject. She had been bought a light up globe a few birthdays ago but couldn't ever remember seeing a place called Atalan on it. In fact, she had never heard of the place, or had she? Something was bugging her, something at the back of her mind. Hang on a minute; it was as if a lightbulb went off in her head. 'Atalan Adventures' was the name of the book from Grandma's and these two elf-like characters looked just like the pair on the front cover.

That must be it, she thought to herself, she must have sat down to read it on Grandma's favourite comfy chair and fell asleep, and this must all be a dream. Isla rubbed her eyes, but when she reopened them, rather than being stood in Grandma's back room looking out over the fields, she was still surrounded by trees in this mysterious forest. She grabbed the skin on her left forearm and give it a little pinch. "Ow," she squealed. Still nothing.

The little boy standing opposite her rubbed his head. He was now really confused at what he was seeing. Isla grabbed her arm again and this time squeezed the skin even harder. "OWW," she shouted and jumped back in pain.

"Are you ok?" asked the boy who she had fallen onto. He picked himself up off the floor, dusted himself down, and retrieved his hat and placed it back on top of his spikey brown hair. He was dressed exactly the same as the other boy.

"No, I'm not ok. One minute I'm stood in my grandma's house looking at a book, and now I'm here, and I don't even know where here is, talking to a pair of elves, and I just want to go home!" The words tumbled out of Isla's mouth at such a rate it was difficult to make out what she was saying. As she spoke, tears began rolling down her cheeks.

"ELVES! DO WE LOOK LIKE ELVES?!" shouted the angrier of the two boys. Before Isla had chance to reply that yes, they both did indeed look like elves to her, the boy continued.

"Why do people always think we are elves?! How come they get all the recognition, and we get none?! What is so great about elves anyway?! They are lazy and mischievous and work literally a few days a year and have terrible dress sense! We are Unkerdunkies!" he said, patting his chest with pride.

"Elves live the other side of Atalan, just near fairy kingdom," said the boy who she had flattened a few moments ago. Despite the fact Isla had landed on him, he seemed a lot calmer and friendlier than the other one. As he spoke, he pointed off into the distance.

"I'm Fartybubble," he said, holding out his hand. Isla wiped her eyes before replying.

"I'm Isla," she said as she shook the Unkerdunkie's hand.

"And this is my excitable little brother Oliver," he said, gesturing towards his brother who had appeared to have calmed down a little.

Oliver walked over and also shook Isla's hand.

"I know what you're thinking: how come he got the cool name, and I got the daft one?"

It wasn't what Isla had been thinking at all. She was actually wondering why someone would name their child Fartybubble!

Oliver continued, "Old Farty over there was lucky enough to be named after our grandpops, while I was named after some fictional character from some made up story that Father likes to tell. And before you start, I've heard all the jokes about my name."

Isla wasn't really sure what jokes she could make about his name. Fartybubble on the other hand…!

"You said you wanted to go home. Just where exactly is home?" asked Fartybubble.

"I'm from Nantwich," replied Isla, still a little shaken by the current situation she found herself in. The two Unkerdunkies looked at each other and shrugged. They obviously didn't recognise the name of Isla's hometown.

"It's in England," Isla added, just in case Atalan was actually in a different country.

"That rings a bell, is it just north of Volcano Mountain?" asked Fartybubble.

Isla had no idea where Volcano Mountain was, but she was pretty sure it wasn't in England.

"England, as in the UK," said Isla.

Still just blank looks came back her way.

"It's on Earth!" Hearing these words coming out of her mouth felt strange to Isla. She never imagined she would ever have to describe where she lived as being on Earth!

"EARTH," shouted the Unkerdunkies in unison. "But Earth doesn't exist, it's just a mythical

25

place our parents tell us about before we go to bed," added Oliver with a slight snort of derision.

"It does exist because I'm from there," replied Isla defensively. How dare he make fun of her being from Earth, thought Isla? Here she was in some place called Atalan filled with elves and fairies talking to a pair of Unkerdunkies, one of them called Fartybubble, and she never snorted or laughed once!

"I'm sorry. We don't mean to be rude," Fartybubble quickly added, "just that we've never met someone from Earth before. Does this mean you are a hooman?" asked the older of the two Unkerdunkies.

"Human," replied Isla, correcting his pronunciation.

"Hoo-man," Fartybubble tried again saying it slower this time, but still not quite getting it.

"Hu-man," Isla corrected him again.

"Wow, this is amazing. Meeting a real life Hooman from Earth is unbelievable. You need to tell us all about it. I want to hear about the schoolboy wizard, the old ladies who go around stealing precious jewels, and the blue hedgehog who can run really fast."

Isla didn't bother correcting Fartybubble for a third time. It also appeared that his entire knowledge of Earth was based on children's fiction and computer games. Before Isla had chance to reply, Oliver butted in.

26

"I think before we hear any fascinating stories about Earth there is one other thing we should do…. RUN!" he shouted, pointing over Isla's right shoulder as he did.

She turned around to see what he was pointing at. On the other side of the forest, she could make out five creatures coming through the sun's haze. From this distance, she couldn't make out exactly what they were. They looked dog-like although much larger, possibly the size of a cow or a bull. Their black fur shimmered in the sunlight as they moved as a pack through the forest towards Isla and the two boys. The animals were moving slowly, almost as if they were stalking their prey, but after a few steps, their speed picked up, and they broke into a run. Now they were moving and moving FAST!

They may have been the size of a cow, but they moved like greyhounds. Isla guessed by the reaction of the Unkerdunkies that they were not coming to play, so she quickly turned on her heels and raced after the already fleeing boys. With her much longer legs and bigger strides, it didn't take her long to catch them up.

As she got almost level with Fartybubble, he stumbled, his foot catching on a root of a large tree. He fell to the ground hitting the forest floor with a loud thump. Isla immediately came to a stop to help the fallen Fartybubble as Oliver raced onwards. He hadn't noticed his brother had taken a fall. His head was down, and his arms were pumping as he sprinted away towards safety.

Isla knelt down beside the once again prone Unkerdunkie, looking back towards the approaching pack as she did so. They were getting closer by the second, churning up the ground as they sprinted through the forest in a V-shaped formation.

From this distance, Isla could see just how powerful these beasts were. Their shoulders and legs were packed full of muscle that shimmered under their dark fur as they gracefully moved through the forest towards their intended prey. The sounds of snarling and gnashing of jaws grew louder and louder; whatever they were after, it didn't appear to be a game of fetch, Isla thought to herself as she grabbed Fartybubble's arm and urged him to get up.

"COME ON, GET UP, WE NEED TO GO!" Isla shouted, her voice shaking as she did, as the panic started to set in. She could feel her heart beating so quickly, she thought it was literally going to come out of her chest. Fartybubble cried out in pain as he reached down to his ankle.

"I don't think I can, it hurts so much."

Isla could feel the forest floor vibrating as the thundering beasts grew closer. There was only one thing for it; she grabbed the fallen Unkerdunkie and hoisted him off the floor and over her left shoulder. She was surprised how light he felt, nowhere near as heavy as Jessica, her three year old cousin who she picked up from time to time.

Fartybubble instinctively wrapped his arms around her and held on for dear life as she set off at more of a fast walk than a run. Oliver had come to a stop up ahead and was now urging them towards him. He was stood on some kind of contraption, although Isla wasn't sure what it was.

It appeared to have a wooden platform that was partially covered by the leaves on the floor. Attached to each of the four corners of the platform were ropes that joined together via a large metal ring to create a pyramid shape. Another thicker rope was looped through the metal ring and went up into the trees and disappeared within the canopy. Oliver was holding onto the main rope above him with his right hand and using his left arm to wave frantically towards the onrushing pair.

"COME ON, COME ON, YOU ARE ALMOST HERE," cried Oliver.

Isla wasn't sure what here was or how stepping foot onto this piece of apparatus was going to help, but she didn't really have any other options at the moment. She didn't dare turn round to see how close the mysterious beasts were. She knew they weren't far behind, as the sound of their gnashing was now almost deafening, and the smell of their breath had now hit her nostrils. Her eyes were completely focused on Oliver as she stumbled the last few steps to reach the wooden platform. As soon as her feet had made contact with it, Oliver reached up with both hands and gave the large rope a massive tug. As he did so, the strange device jerked up off the floor and raised up into the air, swinging wildly as it went; so much so that Isla almost fell backwards off it.

"HOLD TIGHT," Oliver commanded although Isla really didn't need telling. She reached out with her right hand and grabbed one of the support ropes. Fartybubble did the same with his right hand, grabbing the rope on the opposite side while using his other arm to still hold on tightly to Isla.

As the trio were lifted up towards safety, chaos erupted below as the snarling beasts jumped up, pawing and snapping at the underside of the platform causing it to swing and shake even more vigorously. Isla grabbed the rope even tighter. As she did so, she could feel Fartybubble's grip around her do the same. It was like being on a fairground ride that her dad enjoyed taking her on whenever the fair came into town, although there wasn't any danger of falling off them and becoming lunch for a hungry cow dog, or whatever those creatures below were called.

As the platform was pulled higher into the canopy of the trees, the swinging and shaking started to subside, and the barking creatures became five small dots on the forest floor. Finally, the lift like device reached its destination and came to a stop with a creek and a groan. The swinging had finally stopped, and Isla could release her vice-like grip of the ropes and let the colour come back into her fingers. She gently lowered Fartybubble down onto the platform floor being careful of his ankle. He gingerly let go of his grip around Isla's neck and let out a slight wince as he stood up on his own without any support.

Oliver hopped off the lift that had carried them to safety and onto another wooden platform. This one was much larger than the one Isla was still stood on, and it was attached to the trunk of the tree and ran all the way around it.

Isla couldn't believe what she was seeing. It was like an entire village built high up in the trees. There must have been fifteen to twenty of these large platforms built around the trunks of nearby trees with rope bridges joining them together. Cut into the trunks of the trees were huts which must be where the Unkerdunkies lived, thought Isla?

As she scanned her surroundings, she caught sight of Oliver out the corner of her eye. He was hopping around like mad, swaying his hips from side to side and swinging his arms about. Isla had seen this move many times before in the playground of her school. Surely the Fortnite craze hadn't reached Atalan because it certainly looked like Oliver was doing the orange justice dance!

"What a rush! That was so cool how we outran those bullhounds," he cried ecstatically while doing his victory dance.

So, that was what those creatures were called, thought Isla to herself, bullhounds and not cowdogs!

"How awesome was that, hey, bro?" Oliver said as he slapped his older brother on the back, a bit harder than maybe he had meant to as it almost knocked Fartybubble off the platform and back down to the awaiting bullhounds below. Fartybubble steadied himself and then stepped off the lift to join his younger brother before turning to Isla. He held out his hand and helped her off the suspended platform and onto more solid ground.

"You saved my life back there. Thank you so much. I am now in your debt," Fartybubble's voice trembled slightly as he spoke to Isla.

He was obviously still shook up, either from the near miss with the bullhounds or the back slap from his brother which had almost sent him plummeting. His once rosy cheeks were now white and pale, and sweat glistened off his brow under his crumpled hat that now had a few leaves and twigs sticking out of it after his earlier fall. Before Isla had a chance to respond, a voice boomed through the trees.

"WHERE HAVE YOU TWO BEEN!?"

"Oh no, it's Father," said Oliver in a hushed voice. "Please don't tell him we were in the forest away from the camp; otherwise, we will be in big trouble."

As Oliver spoke, Isla looked over his shoulder towards where the booming voice had come from. She spotted a figure striding purposely across one of the rope bridges and heading towards the trio. He was a little bit taller than the boys but not by much and was still a piece shorter than Isla. He appeared much older, though, with a long greying beard that was down to his chest and grey bushy hair that was escaping out from under his hat.

He wore very similar attire to the boys, although his outfit seemed a little grander. He wore a red cape around his broad shoulders that flowed down his back, and his hat was far more decorative than both Oliver's and Fartybubble's with brightly coloured feathers adorning it. Around his neck was a necklace of some sort, a piece of red ribbon attached to what appeared to be a giant seashell.

"What have I told you two about going down into the forest without letting an elder know?"

"We didn't go far from the base of the tree. I promise, Father. We just nipped down to pick some mojo berries and...."

The younger Unkerdunkie's sentence was cut short as his father stepped off the rope bridge, and onto the platform that Oliver was stood on, and laid eyes on the stranger in his camp for the first time.

"WHO ON ATALAN IS THIS?!" He bellowed, pointing his right hand directly towards

33

Isla in case there was any confusion in terms of who he was talking about.

"Father, this is Isla. She is from Earth. We found her wandering below near the house tree," Oliver answered before Isla even had chance to.

As soon as the words had left Oliver's mouth, his father shot his head around towards him as if his son had yanked his beard. His face was red with anger.

"EARTH, EARTH!! WHAT HAVE I TOLD YOU ABOUT THE UNKERDUNKIE WHO CRIES BULLHOUND?!" His voice was even louder now. In fact, Isla wasn't sure how someone quite so small could create such a sound.

"THERE IS NO SUCH PLACE AS EARTH," he continued. "IT IS JUST A MADE UP PLACE, A PLACE FOR BEDTIME STORIES. I'VE TOLD YOU BEFORE ABOUT YOUR IMAGINATION AND HOW IT WILL GET YOU INTO TROUBLE."

"Oliver is telling the truth this time, Father," said Fartybubble, coming to his brother's defence.

"Isla is from Earth. She is a hooman," he continued

"Human," whispered Isla under her breath.

"And she saved…" Fartybubble paused mid-sentence. He wanted to tell his father how Isla had rescued him from a pack of hungry bullhounds but knew if he did so, he and Oliver would be in trouble for venturing into the forest and away from the safety of their camp.

He shuffled his feet and looked down at the ground, not wanting to make eye contact with his father as he told him what had happened.

"She saved me from a pack of bullhounds. We hadn't gone far into the forest, I promise, Father, and the bullhounds came right up to our tree."

His father stood there in silence. A look of confusion had spread across his face as he tried to take in what had just been said. He had read his children stories of adventure from this far off land called Earth for many years, but that was all they were, stories written by the elder Unkerdunkies. He never believed they were any more than that, though, just made up stories. Yet here before him stood a stranger who claimed to be from this fictional land.

"Is this true, are you actually from Earth?" the elder Unkerdunkie asked Isla, his voice much softer now and slightly shaky.

"Yes, I am," Isla replied, nodding her head.

"This is a miracle. We must tell the village," as the boy's father spoke, he lifted the shell-like necklace to his mouth and gently blew into it.

Nothing seemed to happen, or at least Isla couldn't hear anything, but all of a sudden, the camp came to life. Unkerdunkies appeared from everywhere: men, women, and children all dressed the same and all roughly the same height, although some were even smaller than the three Isla had met so far. They came from out of huts, climbed down from trees, and came up on lifts like the one Isla and the boys had arrived on. In a matter of seconds, the platform that had once been occupied by three Unkerdunkies and a human was packed full of miniature people. It was like a sea of red and green with every pair of eyes focused firmly on Isla.

There were gasps all around, followed by whispering and pointing as the new arrivals tried to figure out just who or what stood before them. After a few seconds, the boys' father raised his right fist into the air and the entire village fell into silence. He held his hand up for a few seconds before slowly lowering it back down and breaking the silence once again with his booming voice.

"FELLOW VILLAGERS, I WOULD LIKE TO INTRODUCE YOU TO A VERY SPECIAL GUEST. THIS IS ISLA, AND SHE IS FROM EARTH."

As soon as he mentioned the E word, the whole village let out a gasp in unison followed by a lot of hushed chatter. After a few seconds of this, the arm was once again raised bringing order and quiet back into the village.

"MY BRAVE SONS FOUND HER IN THE FOREST AND RESCUED HER FROM A PACK OF BLOODTHIRSTY BULLHOUNDS," he continued, bringing more gasps from the on-looking villagers.

Oliver and Fartybubble shot each other a look of surprise and bewilderment. They had gone from fearing the wrath of their father to him basically announcing them as heroes. Fartybubble sheepishly turned to Isla and held his hands up and shrugged his shoulders. He knew full well that if anyone was a hero around here, it was Isla, but now wasn't the time to point that out to his father and the entire village. Isla too remained silent even though part of her wanted to shout out that it had been her who had saved Fartybubble and not the other way around, but as she was here in a mysterious land surrounded by Unkerdunkies, she thought it was wise to keep her mouth shut at least for now!

"AS THE LEADER OF THIS VILLAGE, I, THUNDERBUM, WOULD LIKE TO OFFER YOU OUR WARMEST WELCOME."

Isla almost erupted into a fit of giggles when she heard that Oliver's and Fartybubble's father was called Thunderbum! There seemed to be a pattern emerging here when it came to naming Unkerdunkies. Luckily, she was able to bite her lip and remain silent, the only tell-tale sign that she had found the name amusing were her shoulders going up and down as she laughed internally.

"I'M SURE WE ALL HAVE LOTS OF QUESTIONS FOR YOU, SUCH AS HOW DID YOU GET HERE, WHY ARE YOU HERE, AND

37

DO YOU KNOW THE QUEEN? BUT FOR NOW, THOSE CAN WAIT. AS IS CUSTOM FOR OUR VILLAGE, WE WELCOME ALL GUESTS WITH A TRADITIONAL UNKERFEST!"

As soon as the last word left Thunderbum's lips, the whole entire village erupted with whoops and cheers. Hats were taken off and thrown into the air and feet were stamped on the wooden floor creating a thunderous sound that caused Isla to fear a little for her safely as the entire platform started to rock. She had visions of it collapsing and sending everyone falling into the forest.

"TAKE ISLA TO THE VILLAGE SQUARE AND LET THE FESTIVITIES BEGIN," boomed Thunderbum.

Isla looked over to Oliver and Fartybubble and got a nod and a smile back from both of them. Whatever an Unkerfest was, it seemed to be popular around here.

The next thing Isla knew, she was surrounded by around six or seven of the villagers who were grabbing at her arms and legs trying to lift her off the ground and carry her away. They were all cheering and laughing while they were doing it, so Isla didn't feel in any particular danger. It felt more like she was some kind of returning hero or as if she had just scored the winning goal in the World Cup final and she was being carried in celebration.

Unfortunately, due to her size compared to these little people, they only managed to lift her

38

high enough so that her feet were only slightly off the ground; in fact, after a couple of steps, her trainers were actually dragging along the floor, and the Unkerdunkies who were carrying her were all starting to puff and pant.

"It's ok, I can walk, but thank you," said Isla politely, easing herself out of the grasp of the struggling crowd. They all looked at her with enormous smiles of relief that they didn't have to carry her any further.

"Follow me," said one of the Unkerdunkies who had been trying to carry her as he grabbed hold of her hand and led her through the village, skipping as he went. He looked to be slightly older than Isla, but again, it was difficult to tell as he was much smaller than her. He was wearing what was obviously their traditional clothing, the green tunic and stripy green trousers complete with hat that was perched on top of a mound of ginger hair. As they moved through the village over rope bridges and past tree huts, the Unkerdunkies chanted, "Unkerfest, Unkerfest."

"What is an Unkerfest?" enquired Isla, but the Unkerdunkie either couldn't hear her because of all the chanting or chose to ignore her as no reply was forthcoming.

They crossed another small rope bridge and came to a stop on a large wooden square that was suspended between four large trees. In the middle of the square was a mound of stones in which a small fire burnt brightly inside it and all around the edge of the square were logs that had been cut up to make seats. Isla was ushered over to one of these log seats and sat down while the entire square started filling up in front of her. Unkerdunkies were everywhere, singing, dancing and doing flips and cartwheels; it felt like being at a circus.

Through all this activity came an older looking lady who approached Isla carrying a mug of something. She was dressed very similar to Thunderbum with the red cape flowing behind her although she didn't have a shell hanging from her neck. She had medium length brown hair that was starting to turn grey and wore little black rimmed glasses.

"I'm Trumpoftenitchybottom," said the lady, smiling and handing Isla the mug. "But you can call me Jules."

Isla smiled and thanked her as she took the steaming hot drink. The mug was wooden and decorated with lots of intricately carved leaves. The liquid inside was dark purple and bubbling. It didn't look like the most appealing of drinks that Isla had ever had. Her facial expression must have portrayed her thoughts to Jules.

"This drink is an Unkerdunkie speciality made from the sagerberry and will help you relax. Drink it my dear, it tastes better than it looks."

Holding the mug with both hands, Isla slowly brought it up to her lips. She gave it a blow to help cool it down and breathed in its aroma. The smell reminded her of candyfloss and since she was a big fan of that, she thought she would give it a try. She took a small sip and felt the hot liquid run all the way down her throat and create a warm sensation in her belly. It was one of the nicest things she had ever tasted, like all her favourite sweets mixed into one and made into a liquid. Her face lit up, and she took a big gulp of it almost burning her mouth in the process. Jules happily watched on as Isla guzzled the entire drink down, wiping her mouth with her sleeve when she had finished.

"I'm glad you enjoyed our little drink. Enjoy the rest of the Unkerfest." And with that, Jules took the mug and left, leaving behind a long line of Unkerdunkies that had formed behind her, all bearing gifts of some sort for Isla, and with every gift came a question.

"Have you met the Queen?" or "Do you know Harry Potter?" as well as "Is the Earth really flat?"

She was given plenty of food and drink, and with each gift, the Unkerdunkies were insistent she try it. She tasted everything until she came to something that resembled a pancake. She took one bite and immediately spat it out, it tasted like rotten fish. The poor Unkerdunkie who had given it to Isla looked mortified, but luckily, she was able to spare his feelings by telling him she was full and felt a little sick from all the excitement of the day's

41

events. After this, any other food item was gratefully accepted and then put to one side. She didn't think spitting food on any more Unkerdunkies was the way to make a good first impression.

As well as edible gifts, she was also given an Unkerdunkie hat and what looked like a hand knitted blanket. The gifts kept coming, and it looked like the line was neverending when, all of a sudden, it stopped.

The line parted, and the Unkerdunkies all made their way to the edge of the platform and sat down on the floor. Thunderbum stood in the centre with the giant seashell to his mouth. He waited until all the Unkerdunkies had sat down and everyone was quiet before he spoke.

"Isla, I hope you are enjoying the Unkerfest so far. As you can see, we are all excited to meet you and find out about where you are from and how you got here. Would you like to tell us about how you came to be in Atalan?"

Isla looked out at the sea of tiny Unkerdunkies all waiting to hear what she had to say, tiny eyes all focused on her. Isla cleared her throat and slowly started talking. She told them about arriving at her grandma's and how she had found the box with a book in it called 'Atalan Adventures' and then how she had seemingly fallen into the page and had ended up here.

As she spoke, she could feel herself starting to get upset. The realisation was starting to set in. She was in a strange land on her own, and she had no idea how she was going to get back home to see her family. Before she knew it, the tears came, and she found herself sobbing uncontrollably. The entire village stared back at her in silence, no one really knowing what to say or do.

After a few moments, a commotion amongst a group of Unkerdunkies broke the silence. Something was causing them to stand up and move to one side. Isla looked up to see what was causing this. Through the crowd, something was moving, and it was heading towards her. Whatever it was, it was small, as it was managing to scurry under the legs of the now stood up Unkerdunkies.

As Isla looked on, she saw something appear through the crowd. It looked like the head of the mop that Grandma often used to clean the kitchen floor. The only difference was this one had legs, six to be precise, and eyes, a pair of big blue ones that were locked onto Isla. The six legged mop head moved swiftly across the floor and jumped up into Isla's lap. It felt soft and warm and now she was up close with it, she could see how cute it was. Its face reminded her of a pug, and it was very affectionate. It buried its head into Isla's chest and then started licking at her face. Its little tongue felt wet and slightly furry.

As it licked Isla, she started to laugh, and the thoughts of home briefly vanished as this little creature fussed her. As Isla laughed and giggled, the onlooking Unkerdunkies did the same, breaking into laughter, cheering and applauding, pleased that their guest was now happy.

"Mopsy, come here Mopsy, you naughty furble," the voice came from Fartybubble as he made his way through the crowd and over to Isla.

"I'm sorry, Isla, she can sense when Unkerdunkies are sad and likes to comfort them and it seems she can do the same with Hoomans."

"That's ok, she's lovely. What is she?" said Isla still giggling away as her face was given a thorough wash by Mopsy.

"This is Mopsy, and she is my pet furble. Do you not have furbles on Earth?"

Isla shook her head as Fartybubble peeled Mopsy off her.

"Come here, Mopsy, there's a good girl," Fartybubble said as he gently placed her down and took a seat on the floor next to Isla. The rest of the Unkerdunkies followed suit, sitting back down on the floor, and a hush fell over the village until Thunderbum once again broke the silence

"I am sorry to hear about this situation you find yourself in, Isla, and I apologise for causing you upset. If there is anything we can do to help or assist in you getting back home, then we will."

44

"We should ask Wally the Wizard. Let's take her to see Wally," called out Oliver.

"Where's Wally?" asked Isla, turning to Fartybubble.

"He lives deeper in the forest. He is the wizard of Atalan," replied Fartybubble, pointing off somewhere in the distance as he did so.

Oliver was hopping around and waving his arms about as he was obviously getting excited about his idea.

"Me and Farty could take her to see him. It wouldn't take us long to get there. With our forest school knowledge, we could find his place no problem and be back here before you know it."

Thunderbum gave his son a disapproving look and shook his head.

"You and your brother can't go wandering through the forest looking for a wizard. Who knows what lurks out there beyond the village. What kind of responsible father would I be if I let my forty-nine year old son wander deep into the forest?"

Forty-nine?! thought Isla to herself, how do they measure age here, in dog years?!

"But we are brave. Remember, we rescued Isla from the bullhounds. You said so yourself, Father," Oliver protested. His father shot him one of those looks that indicated it was time to be quiet.

"No, Oliver, I've made my decision. Isla, you have obviously had an eventful day. I suggest you rest up for the evening, and we can discuss what we

45

can do to help in the morning. Fartybubble, would you show her to your room? Isla can sleep in there tonight, and you can share with your brother."

Fartybubble nodded to his father and gestured for Isla to follow him. He led her away from the horde of Unkerdunkies, across a rope bridge to a small hut that was carved out of one of the large tree trunks. Oliver followed on after. He kept his head down as he walked, obviously upset that his idea had been rejected by his father.

Once they reached the doorway to the hut, Fartybubble showed Isla inside. She had to duck her head slightly to enter. There wasn't much room inside, and the room was pretty bare; there was a small desk and stool in one corner that had been carved out of wood. On the opposite side of the room was what Isla could only presume was the bed. It looked like a large branch had been hollowed out, and inside it had been stuffed with leaves and material that resembled straw. Isla wasn't very hopeful of a good night's sleep.

"We will let you get some sleep, and we shall see you in the morning," Fartybubble said as he exited the hut.

"Don't worry, we will find a way to get you home," said Oliver from the doorway. And with that, he wished her goodnight and left her to her thoughts.

Isla sat down onto the bed of twigs, leaves, and straw and rested her head in her hands. She didn't think she would get much sleep tonight as she had so much racing through her mind, but as she sat down, a wave of tiredness swept over her. Maybe it was the effect of the drink she had earlier. Whatever it was, her eyes suddenly felt very heavy. She rested her head onto the giant leaf which was her pillow for the night and before she knew it, she was fast asleep.

Chapter 3

Isla's deep sleep was interrupted when she felt a hand on her shoulder. She woke with a start to find Fartybubble and Oliver by her bedside. Fartybubble was gently rubbing her right shoulder to try and wake her. As she shot up out of bed, he put his finger to his lips.

"Sshh. We need to be quiet as to not to wake anyone in the village."

"What is going on?" whispered Isla, rubbing the sleep out of her eyes.

"We are busting you out of here!" said Oliver, trying his hardest in all his excitement to whisper. Isla looked at him confused.

"What do you mean, bust me out?"

"Farty and I have been talking, and we've decided we are going to help you get back home. We are going to take you to see Wally. I'm sure he will be able to help you."

"Really?" asked Isla. Looking at Fartybubble's face, he didn't look so sure about this idea. "Does your father know about this?"

"Look, you saved my brother's life yesterday from that pack of bullhounds, so we are now in your debt. It is Unkerdunkie code that we must repay the favour and help you. Only then will we be even. As for our father, he is a great man, but he is also very protective. Not just of us but the entire village. Ever

48

since his father, our grandpops, went out one day to get some supplies and never came back, he has been like this. When he became the head of the village, he swore that he would protect us all and keep everyone safe. That is why he won't let us or anyone else, for that matter, take you to see Wally." Oliver bowed his head as he finished his story and a look of sadness washed across his face.

"I am so sorry to hear about your grandpops," said Isla. She reached out and rested her hand on Oliver's shoulder. He looked up and smiled at her.

"And that is why we need to take you now while the village is still asleep. We can go and see the wizard and be back before anyone knows we have gone." As Oliver spoke, he jumped up from his kneeling position beside Isla's bed and gestured for her to get up.

"Do you know the way?" asked Isla as she climbed out of her bed.

Oliver pulled out a map from his pocket and nodded, a big smile beaming across his face.

"I managed to take this from our library without anyone seeing. It shows all the important places within the forest including Wally's house."

"You have a library?" said Isla a little surprised.

"Of course. Anyway, enough of the questions, we need to get going," and with that, Oliver turned and disappeared out of the hut.

Isla climbed out of her surprisingly comfy bed and, along with Fartybubble, headed out the hut to catch Oliver up. By now, he was stood by the platform that had carried Isla up to safety and away from the bullhounds. He held a lantern in his right hand while using his left to undo some ropes that held the makeshift lift in place.

When Isla approached, Oliver turned to her and with a big smile said, "Going down, ma'am?" which made him laugh hysterically.

"Sshh. You will wake the village," Fartybubble warned his younger brother.

Oliver nodded in agreement and composed himself before motioning that everyone should step onto the lift's wooden platform. Just then, there was a noise from somewhere within the village. Isla spun round to see what had caused it, thinking that they had been rumbled. Across a nearby rope bridge came a bounding object, not a villager coming to stop them or raise the alarm, but a furry ball of fun.

"Mopsy," whispered Fartybubble as the lovable furble came flying over to them and jumped up into his arms. She gave him a huge lick and then nestled into his chest.

"Look, Oliver, Mopsy wants to come with us," Fartybubble said to his younger brother.

"She can't, unfortunately. She will slow us down, and if she runs off into the forest chasing something and gets lost, then what?" Oliver replied.

Fartybubble looked sadly into Mopsy's big blue eyes that were looking up at him.

"You can't come with us I'm afraid, Mops. You need to stay here and protect the village. We won't be gone long and will be back before you know it," Fartybubble placed the furble onto the floor and patted her head. Mopsy looked up at him and let out a little whimper. Isla looked over to Fartybubble and for a moment thought he was going to cry. She hoped he didn't; otherwise, it might set her off as well.

"Come on, we really must go now," whispered Oliver, ushering everyone onto the lift. With a tug of the rope, the lift slowly started its descent to the forest below. Fartybubble waved goodbye to his beloved pet as she disappeared out of sight.

The lantern lit up the forest with an eerie glow causing shadows to dance and flicker off the trees and bushes that lined the narrow dirt track that the trio were following. Oliver led the way holding the lantern up at arm's length in his right hand while studying the map that he gripped tightly in his left. Fartybubble followed closely behind, his eyes constantly scanning the surroundings.

Every time the wind rustled the leaves or there was some kind of movement in the undergrowth caused by some sort of bug or creature, he would jump and let out a hushed cry of, "What was that?!"

On each occasion, Oliver would reassure him that it was nothing and that they were perfectly safe. Oliver may have been the younger of the two, but he certainly seemed to be the braver and more confident of the pair.

Isla followed closely behind the two brothers, keeping her eyes peeled on the guiding light ahead. She wasn't a big fan of the dark, especially when walking through a forest that caused innocent shapes and sounds to appear far scarier than they should. At home, she would often go to bed with a night light on, but she wasn't going to show any weakness to the boys or let this irrational fear stop her in her quest to hopefully find a way home.

After what seemed like the hundredth time that Fartybubble had jumped and muttered the words, "What was that?!" his brother turned to him.

"Will you get a grip? There is nothing to be afraid of," Oliver spoke firmly but in a hushed tone. "Being out in the dark is the same as being out in the daytime just with less light."

"But that last noise I heard sounded very much like a conkaburrow!" Fartybubble said with a definite shake to his voice. Isla didn't have a clue what a conkaburrow was but guessed she didn't particularly want to meet one deep in a darkened forest.

"Conkaburrows don't live in this part of the forest. Didn't you learn anything at forest school?" asked Oliver.

"Bullhounds then?" inquired Fartybubble. Isla could tell that Oliver was starting to lose his patience with his older brother.

"Bullhounds don't hunt at night. They will all be tucked up in their dens."

"Daggermoths?"

The third question seemed to push Oliver over the edge, and his answer came back with more of a shout rather than the whisper it had previously.

"THERE ARE NO CONKABURROWS, BULLHOUNDS, DAGGERMOTHS, KING BETTLES, FLYING THROWBACKS OR ANYTHING ELSE YOU CAN THINK OF IN THIS PART OF THE FOREST! WE ARE PERFECTLY SAFE AS LONG AS WE STICK TO THE PATH AND AVOID ANYYYYYYYYYYYYYYY…!!"

All of a sudden, Oliver's sentence was cut short as something grabbed hold of him and pulled him off the path causing him to drop the lantern. It fell to the floor, landing on its side and illuminating the floor but throwing the surrounding forest into darkness.

Fartybubble let out a scream followed by the usual, "WHAT WAS THAT," although this time shouted at the top of his voice rather than a whisper. Isla froze, almost too frightened to move. She didn't have a clue what was going on. She could hear Oliver off to her right hand side. It sounded like a struggle was taking place as he shouted out, "LET

53

GO OF ME!" but she couldn't see much in the darkness.

She forced herself to move, grabbing the lantern off the floor and holding it up in Oliver's direction. The flame illuminated him, and it appeared as if he was almost floating in mid-air, his feet a good distance off the ground. As Isla looked, she could see that something was wrapped around his body, and whatever it was, seemed to be dragging him deeper into the forest.

"A V-v-v-vinecatcher has got him," stuttered Fartybubble who appeared frozen to the spot.

Isla could now make out that Oliver seemed to have got himself entangled in the vines of a nearby tree although these didn't seem to be the normal kind of vines Isla was used to. These appeared to be alive, moving freely like the tentacles of an octopus. The one that had got hold of Oliver was wrapped tightly around his waist and wasn't letting go as he tried to prise it off. When this didn't work, he started punching it and thrashing his legs around, but if anything, it seemed to make the vine grip him even tighter.

"IT'S GOING TO EAT MY LITTLE BROTHER," cried Fartybubble in absolute panic.

"Eat him?!" Isla responded in shock and surprise. How on earth could a tree eat an Unkerdunkie?! Yes, it appeared to have vines that seemed to be alive and moved like giant fingers, but how could it possibly eat anything or anyone?!

54

Just then, Isla got her answer as the trunk of the vinecatcher contoured into a face. Two giant white eyes with fiery red pupils popped open followed by a huge mouth in the centre of the tree with jagged pieces of bark that created razor-sharp like teeth. This was where Oliver was heading as the vinecatcher reeled the little Unkerdunkie in like a fisherman reeling in a catch.

Isla turned to Fartybubble, but he was still playing a solo game of musical statues without the music. His face was as white as the snow, and it appeared that sheer terror had made him unable to act; if anyone was going to rescue Oliver, it was down to Isla to do something and do something fast.

She looked around to see if there was anything she could use to free Oliver before he became tree fodder, but the only thing she had was the lantern which she was holding. Of course, the lantern, thought Isla as an idea sprung into her head. It might not work but it was the only idea she had.

To execute it, though, she needed to get closer to the vinecatcher without becoming its second meal of the day. She darted off the dirt track and through the undergrowth; as soon as she had, a vine came swooping down towards her. She ducked and sidestepped underneath it, and it sailed safely overhead. All those games of touch rugby at school and being the class champion at bulldog had paid off. She was nimble and agile on her feet as she weaved and stepped past two more flailing vines as she got closer to the trunk. Oliver was only a few metres away from the trunk of the vinecatcher now, and its mouth was wide open ready for its midnight feast.

Isla came to a stop directly opposite the vinecatcher's wide open mouth and steadied herself. She didn't have long before another vine would make a swipe for her. She held the lantern's handle tightly in her right hand and give it a little swing. She hoped that the flickering flame wouldn't go out on her. She held her breath and after one more swing let go of the lantern and sent it soaring through the air towards its intended target.

"BULLSEYE!" Isla shouted in delight as the lantern disappeared inside the gaping hole of the vinecatcher's mouth.

As it flew inside, the monstrous tree slammed its mouth shut, bringing its razor-sharp teeth together smashing the lantern into tiny pieces as it did so. Isla held her breath, hoping her idea would work but nothing seemed to have happened. Oliver was still being reeled in and getting closer to becoming a tasty snack by the second, and the vinecatcher appeared to have consumed the lantern without any side effects.

All of a sudden, the tree's eyes bulged wide open like two giant saucers. It instantly reminded Isla of the cat and mouse cartoon she used to love and how their eyes would pop out of their heads with shock or in pain after being hit over the head with a frying pan! Smoke billowed out of the tree's mouth as the tiny flame from the lantern's candle had set fire to the inside of its trunk. The vinecatcher opened its mouth wide and let out a painful shriek accompanied by a fireball which almost singed poor Oliver's bum!

Isla looked on in terror. It appeared her idea had backfired. The vinecatcher's grip on Oliver hadn't loosened at all, and now, instead of being eaten, he was in danger of being burnt alive. He was like a marshmallow on a stick that was about to be cooked on a campfire.

Another shriek came from the vinecatcher as the fire took hold in its stomach causing it a serious case of heartburn. Another flame shot out from its mouth causing Oliver to let out a cry as he felt the heat on the back of his legs. He kicked and squirmed as hard as he could trying to free himself from the vine's vice-like grip.

As the fire ripped through the vinecatcher's trunk, it thrashed its vine like arms around in pain causing it to loosen its grip momentarily on Oliver. This was the opportunity the little Unkerdunkie needed. He wiggled himself free and slipped through the vine and landed feet first on the floor as agile as a cat.

The moment he hit the ground, the vinecatcher let out another huge fireball that set alight the vine that just seconds ago had been holding Oliver prisoner. Oliver didn't waste any time; as soon as he landed on the floor, he was up and sprinting away from the flaming tree. As he darted past Isla, he grabbed her by the hand and pulled her after him.

"COME ON, LET'S GO!" he shouted.

The pair stumbled through the undergrowth, the flames from the burning vinecatcher lighting up the way. They made it back onto the dirt track where Fartybubble was still standing, his hands held tightly over his eyes, not daring to look.

"COME ON, BRO, LET'S GO," Oliver shouted as he grabbed his older brother's hand.

Holding onto both Isla and Fartybubble, Oliver raced off down the dirt track, deeper into the darkened forest, leaving the burning vinecatcher far behind them. Soon, the trio couldn't see anything. The only lantern they had was gone, and the light from the burning tree was now just a distant glow behind them. Fartybubble tugged at his brother's arm and brought them all to a stop. He slumped to the ground puffing and panting trying to catch his breath.

"We need to stop. We can't see where we are going and could easily run into another vinecatcher or worse," Fartybubble's voice was shaking with fear.

Oliver stood bent over with his hands on his knees trying to catch his breath after the sprint through the forest and the fact he had almost become a vinecatcher's snack.

After a few deep breaths, he stood up and replied, "What a rush! That was so cool. Isla, where did you learn to throw like that!?" Isla smiled and felt herself blush.

"Cool! Are you kidding me? You were almost eaten by a vinecatcher!" Fartybubble replied before Isla had chance to. He certainly didn't have the same outlook on what had just happened as his brother.

"Nah, it was never going to eat me. I was always going to escape. I'm like a furble, I have twenty lives! But you're right, bro, we can't carry on in the dark; otherwise, we are just going to get lost. We need to wait until first light before we continue, plus I've dropped the map," Oliver gave a shrug of his shoulders.

"What do you mean you've dropped the map?" Fartybubble asked angrily.

"Yeah, it fell out of my hand when the pesky vinecatcher grabbed me. But don't worry, I can find the way to Wally's in the daylight. We will just need to wait a while here before we carry on."

"W-w-wait h-h-here?" Fartybubble stuttered.

"Well, yes, we can't carry on in the dark. You said so yourself, and we can't go back to the village. We will wait until first light and then go and see Wally. If we are quick, we can still get back before anyone is up." Oliver slumped to the floor and made himself as comfy as possible.

Since it appeared they wouldn't be going anywhere soon, Isla did the same and sat down onto a nearby log with her elbows resting on her knees and her head in her hands. She took a couple of deep breaths as she tried to get her breathing back to normal after the mad sprint through the forest and the near miss with the vinecatcher.

She fidgeted on the log as she tried to get comfy, but something was sticking into her. She reached into her back pocket and pulled out her phone that she had sat on. A quick press of the home button lit the screen up and she was relieved to see she hadn't damaged it. Happy in the knowledge that it was still in perfect working order, she went to put it back into her pocket but then stopped herself. An idea flashed into her head.

A quick finger swipe and touch of the screen and a small but bright light from the phone's torch illuminated the forest. Fartybubble and Oliver both let out a gasp in amazement at this little rectangular object that was producing more light than the lantern had ever done.

"I forgot I had my phone in my pocket," said Isla sheepishly.

"I don't know what that is, but what are we waiting for? We now have light that can guide us to Wally's, so let's go," said Oliver, beckoning to Isla to lead the way.

"And you're sure you can find the place without the map?" asked Fartybubble.

"Of course, I can. I memorised the route. We just continue along this path until we come to a clearing with a large tree in the middle, and the house is just beyond that."

"Oh, so we are looking for a clearing and a large tree in the middle of a forest?" answered Fartybubble with a hint of sarcasm in his voice.

"Look, bro, when have I ever let you down?"

Fartybubble didn't answer, although his expression seemed to suggest his brother had let him down on a number of occasions.

The trio set back off through the forest with Isla leading the way this time with her phone light guiding them. They proceeded with caution, making sure that they stayed in the middle of the path and away from the undergrowth and any wandering vines. They walked in silence apart from the occasional whisper from Oliver to keep going straight on.

Isla didn't know how long they had been walking, but soon there wasn't any need for the torch light as morning started to break, and daylight started to seep through the canopy. With the darkness starting to disappear, Fartybubble had a different reason to panic.

"It's getting light, and we haven't even got there yet. We will never be back before Father is up. We are going to be in so much trouble."

"We are almost here. Trust me, we can still make it back before anyone knows we are missing," Oliver answered, sounding confident.

"Do you even know where we are? We've been following this path for ages and no sign of this clearing. I bet we are lost and...."

"We are here," said Oliver proudly, before his brother could complete his sentence.

He pointed ahead to a large clearing where the undergrowth and trees fell away to leave a large space of lush green grass with just one solitary tree standing proudly in the middle. It looked a little out of place to Isla, like someone had picked it up and plonked it there, smack bang in the middle. Isla starred at it.

It wasn't very big but there was something about it. Its branches were covered in brightly coloured leaves of greens, reds, and yellows, and it seemed to shimmer and glisten in the early morning sun. It looked almost magical, Isla thought to herself, and she found herself struggling to take her eyes off it until the sound of Fartybubble snapped her out of her gaze.

"Are you sure this is the right clearing?"

"Yes," Oliver replied with conviction.

"Why?" questioned his brother.

"Because of that," Oliver pointed beyond the tree and towards the far side of the clearing where you could just make out a small building tucked back behind the treeline. It was well hidden amongst the undergrowth and was partially covered by bushes and the hanging branches of nearby trees. If it wasn't for grey smoke that was blowing through the trees and into the clearing, obviously coming from the building's unseen chimney, you could have easily walked right past it without knowing it was there.

"And are you sure that's the right building?"

Oliver replied with a grunt and a nod of his head.

"Why?" questioned Fartybubble.

Oliver turned to his brother, smiled and then pointed down towards the ground. Fartybubble turned around to see what he was pointing at, and there, coming out of the ground, was a stick that had a piece of bark attached to the top of it which had been carved into the shape of an arrow and pointed towards the clearing. On the arrow was written, "To Wally's House," in red paint. Fartybubble carefully read the sign and then reread it, as if he was reading a novel instead of three words crudely painted onto a piece of bark.

He clearly didn't like the thought of his brother being right. Once he was satisfied that this was indeed the right clearing and the right house, he turned back round to his brother who by now was grinning like a Cheshire cat.

"Shall we go?" said Oliver as he made his way across the clearing with Isla closely behind and Fartybubble bringing up the rear.

It didn't take the trio long to reach the edge of the clearing where they came to a stop in front of the wizard's home. The bushes that helped camouflage the house formed an archway with the front door of the property situated just beyond.

Oliver went first, ducking his head as not to snag his hat on a twig or a branch. After his previous meeting with the vinecatcher, he didn't fancy getting caught on a tree again. He reached the front door and waited for his two companions to join him.

The door, which had obviously once been a bright red, was now covered in moss and much of the paint had flaked off. In the middle of the door was a large golden lion's head door knocker. Isla spotted this straight away and was taken aback. It looked just like the one her grandma had at Willow cottage. For a moment, it was almost like she was back there, stood outside with her parents waiting for her grandma to open the door and invite them in. Oliver's gentle tap on her shoulder brought her back to reality.

"Do you want to do the honours?" he said, gesturing towards the door knocker.

Isla smiled and nodded before reaching up and grabbing the lion's head and giving it a loud knock. She stepped back and held her breath as she waited for the door to be opened.

Chapter 4

After what felt like hours to Isla but in reality was only a few seconds, there was a sound from the other side of the door: a rattling of keys followed by the creaking of old wood as the door slowly opened. Stood in the doorway was who Isla presumed to be Wally as he was dressed just how Isla imagined a wizard would look. If she had to describe a wizard to someone or draw a picture of one, the person here in front of her was exactly what she would do. She was pretty sure if she googled wizard, then somebody resembling Wally would come up.

He was small in height and dressed head to toe in purple. On his feet, he wore purple ankle boots that were almost met by the long flowing purple gown that covered his entire body. On his head was the obligatory wizard hat, again purple in colour apart from the bright yellow stars that covered it. He had a long white beard that grew almost down to his boots. In his right hand, he held a large set of keys, and in his left hand, he completed the wizard look with a long thin wand that looked like it had been expertly carved out of wood.

He stood in silence in his doorway and scanned the three strangers in front of him. Isla fidgeted not wanting to be the first to speak and not really knowing what to say. She was relieved when Oliver found the courage to break the silence.

"Hi, Wally, I am really sorry to disturb you so early. My name is Oliver, and I've been sent by my father Thunderbum to ask for your help. This is my brother Fartybubble and this is..."

"You must be from Earth. I've been expecting you," Wally said in a deep gruff voice before Oliver had chance to introduce Isla. As the wizard spoke, Isla felt a shiver run down her spine and Goosebumps appear on her arm. How could he possibly know she was from Earth?

Wally turned and disappeared back inside the house, leaving the front door open. Isla stood there along with her two companions, not knowing whether to follow or not.

"Well, are you coming in or not?" shouted the wizard from somewhere inside, "and close the door behind you; you're letting all the heat out."

Isla looked over to Oliver, and he motioned for her to enter first. She stepped nervously through the front door and into what appeared to be the main room of the house and, in fact, possibly the only room of the house. Oliver followed closely behind with Fartybubble bringing up the rear, carefully closing the front door behind him.

The room they had stepped into was very big and seemed much larger than the outside had suggested. Isla looked around the cluttered room trying to take everything in. She was amazed as from the outside, the building had appeared tiny and not much bigger than her parents' garden shed, but now she was inside, the room was almost as big as her school's hall.

All around the room were large bookcases that stood from floor to ceiling overflowing with books of all sizes. On the walls between the shelves were a number of stuffed animals, either framed in glass cases or mounted. Isla had no idea what any of these animals were, and by the looks of some of them, she never wanted to find out.

At the back of the room was the head of a huge animal. It was mounted in pride of place in the middle of the wall. It resembled a pig apart from the massive horns that came out either side of its snout and the razor-sharp fangs that hung from its mouth.

In the middle of the room was a huge wooden table that was full of glasses, beakers, and what looked like test tubes. It reminded Isla of a school science lesson although, by the looks of some of the contents of the beakers, it would be a far more interesting lesson with brightly coloured liquids frothing and spilling out over the top of the containers. One of the test tubes was filled with a liquid that was all of the colours of the rainbow while another fizzed and popped sending smoke up towards the remarkably high ceiling.

To the right of the room stood a large black cauldron that was filled to the brim with a dark looking liquid that was bubbling away to itself and looked in danger of overflowing at any minute and drenching the stone floor it stood on. At the very back of the room was a desk that was littered with papers and a couple of large books and a single chair that had a leg missing yet to Isla's amazement was still standing. She found herself staring at it, trying to work out how it hadn't toppled over. Next to the desk was what Isla assumed to be Wally's bed which consisted of what appeared to be some kind of animal skin blanket covering a concrete-looking slab.

Wally had walked to the back of the room and took a seat on the three legged chair. Isla expected it to collapse as soon as he put his weight on it but, amazingly, it didn't. It didn't even wobble.

"So, Earth child, I'm guessing you've found a book that's brought you to our land. Am I correct?"

Isla was speechless for a moment, not knowing how Wally knew all this. Yes, he was a wizard and wizards were meant to be magical but still. Isla nodded and then cleared her throat before answering.

"Yes, that is correct. I found a book called 'Atalan Adventures' at my grandma's, and somehow I've ended up here. How did you know about the book and that I am from Earth?"

"Let me tell you a story. Once upon a time, there was a powerful wizard who from a young age was obsessed with time travel, teleportation, and moving through different dimensions. He studied it for years until one day he developed a potion that, when sprinkled onto the pages of a book, would bring the pictures to life. You could literally step inside the book and be transported to that place."

"Wow," gasped Isla, Oliver, and Fartybubble in unison.

"Was that the famous wizard known as Merlin?" asked an excited Oliver.

"No, his name was Steve," answered Wally before continuing with his story. "Steve would travel all over to many different worlds and planets. As long as he had a picture of that place, then he could go there. Wherever he went, he would always take a book about Atalan with him so that he could return. On one trip to Earth, though, he met a young lady and fell in love and decided he was going to stay there and start a new life. That and the fact he had misplaced his book so couldn't return home even if he wanted to. He's become a very successful children's entertainer, don't you know. Anyway, that book is the one you found at your grandma's house."

"How do you know all this?" Isla asked, amazed by the story she was hearing.

"Because Steve emailed me and told me."

"EMAIL!?!" shouted Isla, somewhat shocked by Wally's answer.

69

"Yes, of course. This is the 21st century. We no longer communicate by speaking into cauldrons or consulting a crystal ball or rubbing magic crystals together. We use the World Wide Web like everybody else." As Wally spoke, he lifted some of the papers from his desk to reveal a laptop that had been hidden underneath the clutter.

"But you said you had been expecting me. How did you know that?" Isla asked, still somewhat puzzled.

"Because when you opened the book, Steve received a notification that the book had been activated. Once he told me, I knew that someone from Earth was heading to Atalan, and I just guessed they would seek me out to try and help them get back home."

"So, you can help me return home?" asked Isla excitedly.

"No."

For a moment Isla looked at Wally thinking he was joking, hoping that at any moment he would crack a big smile or burst out laughing. But he didn't. He just sat on his three-legged-chair without a hint of any emotion on his face. Isla's heart sank, and she could once again feel the tears welling up in her eyes. It appeared she was destined to stay here forever and never see her family again. How she wished now that she had never opened that stupid book.

"Surely you know how to create the potion needed for teleportation, or if you don't, then can't you just email Steve and ask him how to do it?" Oliver asked. He had noticed that Isla was getting upset and didn't want to give up easily in his quest to help her.

"Yes, of course, I know the potion. But the ingredients needed to make it are not that easy to come by. It's not like you can just pop down to the corner shop or local market and buy the spit of a gurwaver bird."

"Is that what's needed to make it?" asked Fartybubble

"No, I was just giving you an example."

"Surely, if Steve managed to get the stuff needed to make it, then it can't be that hard to come by?" Oliver wasn't prepared to give up without exploring every option.

"The difference between me and Steve, young Unkerdunkie, is that he wanted to visit new places, and I don't. I have no interest in leaving Atalan, so why would I waste my time getting the ingredients needed to make the potion?"

Isla wiped her eyes and took a couple of deep breaths to compose herself. Maybe all wasn't lost just yet.

"Could you tell us what is needed, and we can get the stuff for you?" she asked nervously.

71

Wally looked at her for a second. He gave his long white beard a stroke and then shrugged his shoulders

"I guess so," he replied as he pulled himself off the chair and walked over towards one of the bookcases. He scanned the shelves, trying to find the book he needed. Isla noticed that each shelf was labelled on the end with what was on them, much like you would get at a library. There was a shelf for potions, spells, creatures of Atalan, trees, fungi, and flowers, and one shelf that was labelled crosswords. Surely, it couldn't be the type of crosswords her mum enjoyed doing, Isla thought to herself.

After a few minutes scanning the hundreds of books on the potion shelf, Wally finally pulled out a large blue book that simply had the letter T printed on it in large gold lettering. He gave the front cover a blow and then coughed and wheezed as a large cloud of dust covered him.

"My most used and favourite potions are all saved on the laptop nowadays on PDF files," he said, wiping dust out his beard.

He carried the book over to the table and plonked it down with a thump almost causing the contents from a couple of beakers to overflow. He opened the book and started flicking through the pages, reading out loud some of the potions that were contained inside.

"Tantrum stopper, tantrum starter. Ha-ha, I'm not sure who thought that potion was a good idea," he said shaking his head

"Telekinesis, telepathy, ah…here we go, teleportation." Wally tapped the page with his finger.

"You might want to write this down. There is a fair bit to remember," Wally said, looking up from his book.

Oliver and Fartybubble both checked the pockets of their tunics before patting themselves down as if they would magically discover a hidden notepad and pen. As Isla watched them search frantically for some writing material, she remembered her phone still safely tucked in her back pocket. She pulled it out and went onto her notes.

"Ok, fire away," she said with a smile.

"Nice iPhone," said Wally, giving Isla a nod of appreciation. "Right then. You will need one leaf from a magic tree, a large bag of frothing berries, two feathers from a buzzagon…"

"What's a buzzagon?" interrupted Isla.

"Go and fetch me the book called 'Winged Creatures of Atalan', and I will show you," Wally said, pointing to one of the bookcases behind Isla. She walked over to the shelf labelled 'Creatures of Atalan' and scanned the many books on there. It didn't take her long to find it. She carefully pulled down the thin purple book and took it over to

Wally. He found the page he wanted and then placed the book face up on the table. In the centre of the page was a large picture of a creature. It was green in colour with giant wings and a long scaly tail and it was breathing fire. To Isla it looked just like a…

"A DRAGON!" exclaimed Isla.

Wally laughed and shook his head.

"Ha-ha. No, my child, dragons are mythical creatures that don't exist. This is a buzzagon."

"Does it fly?" asked Isla

"Yes, of course. It is the fastest winged creature in the whole of Atalan." As Wally answered, he held out his arms as if growing wings himself.

"And does it breathe fire?"

"You only have to look at the picture to see that," Wally tapped the book as he answered Isla's question.

"So, how is it any different to a dragon?" Isla asked, holding her arms out in confusion.

"Because dragons do not exist. They are creatures that you Earth folk make up for your fairy tales and farfetched stories of brave knights slaying them. Now, may I continue with the list of ingredients?"

"I don't think there is much point. It's not like we will be going looking for any of this stuff anyway," said Fartybubble, looking around at Oliver and Isla as he spoke.

74

"Why not, bro?" came the reply from Oliver.

"Because, bro, Wally just said we needed two feathers from a buzzagon. A winged beast with massive claws and sharp teeth that flies and breathes fire. I, for one, am going nowhere near one of those."

"It's not like we have to actually pluck the feathers from one. We can just find some that have come loose and fallen to the ground.... can't we?" Oliver turned to Wally, hoping that he was right about this.

"It doesn't matter how you come about the feathers as long as they have come from an actual buzzagon. Now, do you want me to continue with the rest of the potion?"

Oliver and Isla both nodded back to Wally while Fartybubble shook his head vigorously.

"Now, where was I? Ah, yes, two buzzagon feathers, a handful of whiteflower seeds, I might have some of them already," Wally stroked his beard and walked back over to his desk. He pulled a drawer out that was underneath it and rummaged around inside. Eventually, he pulled out a small cloth bag that was tied up with string and brought it back over to the table. He undid the string and emptied the contents into his hand. What came out reminded Isla of sunflower seeds, much like the ones she had used recently in a school competition to see who could grow the largest sunflower. She had finished second behind Rupert Nuttles;

although, there were rumours that Rupert's sunflower had been chemically enhanced since his dad was the manager of a local chemist!

Once Wally was satisfied that there was indeed a handful of seeds, he placed them back in the bag and handed them over to Isla.

"You can have those. Now, what else is left to get. Ah, just one final ingredient: a bottle of goblin brew."

"And what is goblin brew?" asked Isla.

"It is the traditional drink of the goblins," replied Wally.

"So, is that something you can buy from a shop?" asked Isla.

"Ha-ha, no, no, my child. Goblin brew can only be found at the Goblin Kingdom. This is where they make it. The goblins do not sell it to outsiders."

"So, would they give us a bottle if we asked them nicely?" said Isla hopefully.

"Ha-ha-ha no," laughed Wally.

"Goblins don't really like Unkerdunkies," said Oliver with a shrug.

"Goblins don't like anyone," said Fartybubble. "And because of that, it will be impossible for us to get any. I'm sorry, Isla, but the ingredients for the potion are just too dangerous for us to get. We will have to find another way to get you home."

Isla's head dropped, and she stood looking at the floor in silence not knowing what to say. She really didn't know how or even if she would ever get back home and see her family again.

"Come on, bro, I'm sure the three of us together can figure out a way of getting what's needed. Plus, don't forget the Unkerdunkie code, we are in Isla's debt. You owe her for saving you from the hounds, and she assisted me in escaping the vinecatcher. I mean, I would obviously have gotten out of it myself, but she did help a little."

Isla shot Oliver a questioning look but didn't say anything. He was on her side, so it seemed, and she didn't want that to change. Oliver continued his pitch to his brother, trying to convince him that tracking down the items was not only achievable but also a good idea.

"Just think of this as a quest. How often do we play wizards and warriors in the forest and pretend to rescue a fair maiden? We both always want to be the brave warrior." As Oliver said this, Wally cleared his throat to remind the young Unkerdunkie that there was an actual wizard stood in the room.

"No offence, Wally," Oliver hastily added before continuing. "Well, bro, this is your chance to be a brave warrior and go on a real-life mission to help a fair maiden. We will be heroes within the village and be respected. People will call us Fartybubble and Oliver the brave. I mean, it's ok for you because you already have a cool name and no one teases you about it, but what about me? No longer would they be asking me 'would I like some more'; instead, they would be asking me to tell them the tale of the time I helped a human return to Earth and battled buzzagons and goblins. We can do this, bro, I believe in you."

Fartybubble stood in silence thinking about what his brother had said. He looked at his brother and then at Isla and then back to his brother before finally answering.

"I want to help Isla get home. I really do. But even if we could track all this stuff down, it will take us forever. We need to get back home. Father is going to go crazy when he realises we have gone, and if we are any later back, he might banish us from the village altogether."

"He won't banish us. He might ground us for a bit, but he won't banish us. Anyway, it will be fine. He will find the note we wrote him and just think that we left early and took Isla to forest school. We can get all the stuff needed for the potion and get back home before nightfall."

"What you need is a spell that stops time. So, when you get back home it seems like you have only been gone for a few minutes," Wally said with a huge smile on his face.

"Wow, can you do that?" Fartybubble asked.

"Heck, no, but it would be cool if I could!"

The looks Wally got from his three guests made him realise that maybe now wasn't a good time for jokes. He laughed nervously and cleared his throat before he spoke again.

"Look, if you are positive you want to try and do this, then maybe I do have some actual spells and potions that could help you on your way." Wally turned away and walked over to the corner of the room behind where the large cauldron stood.

The shelves here were not full of books but instead were made up of rows of bottles and jars and a label stuck to the front read 'Potions'. After much perusing, Wally picked up one large bottle and one very small glass container about the size of a thimble and brought them back over to the table. The large bottle had a label on it which read 'invisibility', and Wally held it up for everyone to see.

"Does anyone know what this potion will do?" Wally asked to no one in particular.

"Um, turn you invisible?" answered Isla.

"That is right. How did you guess that?" asked Wally in surprise.

"Because it says it on the label," Isla said, pointing to the bottle.

"Oh, I didn't know you could read Atalanian," Wally said with a shrug.

Isla didn't reply. She just looked at the wizard with a slightly confused look on her face.

"If you each take two big gulps of this potion, then you will disappear out of sight for a short amount of time," continued Wally excitedly.

"How will you know the potion has worn off?" questioned Isla.

"Umm… because whoever you are trying to be invisible from will be able to see you again!" answered Wally, a little bit sarcastically for Isla's liking. She was starting to find the wizard more annoying than helpful.

"Yes, I understand that. I meant will you get a sign that the potion has worn off or will you just go from being invisible to being seen again?" Isla asked, managing to hide her frustration.

"Oh, I see what you mean. Yes, you get a tingling feeling in your cheeks just before you go back to normal."

As Wally answered, Oliver burst out laughing uncontrollably at what he had said. Everyone turned to look at him.

"Tingling in your cheeks. Get it?! Like bum cheeks, so tingling in your bum!" Oliver held his belly and wiped tears away from his eyes. Wally just shook his head and carried on with what he was saying.

"Cheeks on your face," Wally touched his face to emphasise his point, "anyway, as I was saying, that one turns you invisible while this one makes you fly." The wizard proudly held aloft the small thimble-sized container as if he was holding up the world cup trophy.

"FLY," gasped Isla and Fartybubble while Oliver was still laughing at his own tingling bum joke.

"Yes, fly. Just a very small sip of this each and you will be able to fly for a short amount of time. Use it wisely, though, as it doesn't last very long at all."

"And how do you know when the potion is about to wear off? And please don't say when you fall out of the sky!" asked Isla

"Umm... when you fall out of the sky. There is no warning with this, I'm afraid. You will quite simply go from flying to falling. So, my advice is fly close to the ground or over something soft. But still, the ability to fly, that's a pretty cool potion don't you think?"

"You haven't got more of the potion, have you? It would be so much quicker to fly around Atalan than walk and then we could get back home before Father realised where we had gone," asked Fartybubble.

Wally shook his head before answering, "To make a container this size of flying potion requires me to get a container that size full of bullhound sweat," Wally pointed to a large glass jar on the table that resembled a fish bowl, "and you know what bullhounds are like."

Fartybubble nodded as he had flashbacks to his encounter with an angry pack of them the previous day.

"Well, yes I can imagine that would be difficult, vicious creatures that they are," he said.

"No, not because they are vicious, bullhounds are quite the opposite. They are playful creatures. They can just come across vicious because they get over-excited when they see people. It is difficult because it takes a lot to make them sweat. It took me a full day of playing fetch with an entire pack of them just to produce this small amount of potion."

"Oh, I see," said Fartybubble, looking a little confused.

Isla quickly butted in before Fartybubble had a chance to realise that what she had done the previous day was rescue him from a pack of creatures that just wanted to play fetch and not rip him limb from limb, meaning that he wasn't in her debt, and he didn't have to help her get home because of some Unkerdunkie code after all.

"That's great, Wally, thank you. I'm sure both of these potions will be a great help in our quest. If that's all, shall we make a move?" she said, gesturing to her two companions that they should get ready to go.

"I have one other thing that will help you on your journey. It's a map that will guide you on your way. Now, where did I put it?" said Wally as he stroked his bead and looked around the room.

He walked over to his desk and searched through the papers on top but didn't find what he was looking for. He pulled a few books off the shelves and gave them a shake to see if anything dropped out but there was nothing. After a few minutes searching, he clicked his fingers and let out an, "Aha," as it dawned on him where whatever it was he was looking for was.

He walked over to one of the bookcases and reached up, standing on his tiptoes, and pulled down a scroll that was tied up with red ribbon. He brought it back over to the table and undid the ribbon and rolled it out, placing a couple of jars on each corner to keep it flat. The scroll was completely blank.

"How will this help us?" asked Isla. She wasn't an expert in maps but knew they normally had more detail on them than this.

"One moment, please, I need to cast a spell," Wally picked up his wand and waved it over the blank sheet.

"Saticus Navicus," he shouted. As he did, the end of the wand lit up and glowed red followed by a bang and a puff of smoke that made Isla and Fartybubble jump. And then, as if by magic, which it obviously was, a red arrow appeared on the scroll seemingly showing the way to go. The map showed the inside of Wally's house and the arrow was pointing towards the front door.

"The map will change as you move and the arrow will point you towards the next nearest item you need for the potion," said Wally with a smile on his face, obviously pleased with his handy work.

"Where is it pointing to now then?" enquired Isla.

"The magic tree outside which you need a leaf from. It's the one in the middle of the clearing."

"I knew it was magic," said Isla under her breath.

Wally picked up the map from off the table and handed it to Isla. He then handed her a large canvas bag with a strap that had been hanging from a hook on the wall.

"What does this do?" asked Isla, wondering what magic was contained inside.

"It will hold all the stuff you get inside. It's a bag, that's what bags do." Maybe on Earth they didn't have such things as bags, Wally thought to himself.

"Well, if that's everything, shall we make a move? We are obviously on a tight schedule to get back," Oliver said. He had finally composed himself and was now ready to set off.

"There is just one more thing you will need to make this work. Once you have got all the items and have brought them back to me, I will need a picture of where you want to go. Without a picture I cannot teleport you," Wally looked over to Isla.

"A picture," Isla said, mainly to herself. She didn't carry any photos with her; the only thing she had with her was her phone. Wait, of course, her phone. She grabbed it out her pocket and went into her photo album. She scrolled through all the selfies until she finally came to what she was looking for. There on the screen was a picture of Isla with her mum, dad and grandma all smiling as they stood outside Willow cottage one lovely summer's day.

"There, that's where I want to go," Isla said excitedly as she pointed to the screen.

"Well, normally the teleport spell is done with a picture in a book, but I guess it will work with a photo on a phone. Only one way to find out."

Chapter 5

After bidding farewell to Wally, the trio left his house and stepped back out into the forest. It was a lovely morning. The sun was shining brightly, and Isla could feel the heat on her face. It really was the perfect day for a quest, she thought to herself. Oliver led the way, once again carrying the map. Isla followed holding the bag containing the potions, and Fartybubble brought up the rear.

Oliver purposely marched across the clearing to the magic tree and carefully picked one of the leaves from it. He handed it to Isla so she could keep it safe in the bag. Once she has placed it safely inside, she put the strap over her head and tucked the bag safely under her right arm.

"Well, that's the first item found. See? This is going to be easy, and we will be home in no time," Oliver said, smiling at his brother. Fartybubble rolled his eyes and tutted. He obviously wasn't as sure as his younger brother.

"Where is the map pointing to now?" asked Isla, craning her neck to try and see what it showed.

The arrow on the map was pointing over towards the right of the clearing where a path disappeared back into the forest. On the top of the map were the words 'frothing berries', indicating what the next nearest item was.

"Frothing berries, I love those. Grandpops used to always bring some back with him from his travels. I've not had any since, well, you know," Oliver looked down at the floor, sadness etched across his face as he remembered his grandpops. His brother placed a hand on his shoulder.

"I love frothing berries as well. Let's go get ourselves some. Maybe we could get a few extra to take back to the village," said Fartybubble. Oliver looked up at his brother and smiled and nodded.

"You're right, come on team, let's go," and with that Oliver led the way into the forest, letting the map guide them towards their second item.

After a short walk under the forest canopy, the map led them through a clearing and out into the open. The sight that greeted them almost took Isla's breath away. It was green as far as the eye could see, rolling hills and fields of lush green grass all around. The sky over the hills was bright blue without a single cloud in it, not that Isla knew if they had clouds or rain in Atalan! It really was a beautiful place, she thought to herself. As she took a moment to take in her surroundings, Oliver continued forward, his eyes fixed on the map.

"Come on, follow me, it's this way, just across this field and over the hill," he said, pointing off into the distance.

The three of them covered the field in no time and were soon at the top of the hill looking down to the other side. The field below had what appeared to be an orchard at the far end. Rows of trees all covered in bright red berries covered the area.

"Frothing berries," exclaimed Oliver proudly.

He shot off down the hill, half running half stumbling. Isla followed on after, taking her time so as not to lose her footing and end up at the bottom of the hill quicker than she wanted. She reached the bottom of the hill safely and turned around to see Fartybubble coming down on his bum.

Once he had joined her, they made their way across the field to join Oliver, who by now had reached the trees. He was jumping up trying to dislodge the berries from the branches, but they were slightly too high and out of his reach.

His next idea was to try and climb one of the trees, but the trunks were very smooth and there was nothing for him to grip onto. Isla stood on her tiptoes and tried to grab one of the berries from a branch but even though she was a fair bit taller than Oliver, she too couldn't reach.

She looked around the floor to see if any of the berries had fallen from the trees, but the only things that were on the ground were twigs and sticks that had obviously fallen from the branches. Isla picked up one of the larger sticks and looked up at the frothing berries hanging above her head. She remembered the times she and her dad would go down to a nearby horse-chestnut tree and spend hours throwing sticks up into the branches trying to knock down the conkers.

She took a step back from the base of the tree and took aim, launching the stick high into the branches. As the stick came crashing back down to the ground, it brought a torrent of berries with it. Oliver stopped trying to climb the tree and turned around to see what the clattering noise was.

"Woo, it's raining berries, hallelujah!" he shouted, running over to pick them up off the ground. He grabbed a handful and passed them over to Isla so she could put them in the bag.

"Get as many as you can. Once the bag is full, then we can have some ourselves and take some back to the village," Oliver shouted, hopping around with excitement.

Isla continued throwing the stick up into the trees until the bag was completely full of berries and there were still plenty left over for her and the boys to try. Oliver picked one up off the floor and gave it a blow and a wipe on his tunic before popping it into his mouth.

"Watch this," he said.

After a couple of chews, he swallowed the berry and then almost immediately let out a huge burp. Isla watched on in amazement; as the sound left Oliver's mouth he was shot up into the air above the treetops. As he started to float back down to the ground, he let out another loud burp and shot back up into the air, laughing as he went.

89

"My turn, my turn!" cried Fartybubble as he raced over to where the berries were lying. He popped a couple into his mouth, and a few seconds later, he too was high up in the air being propelled by gas!

Oliver finally stopped burping and floated safely back down to the ground.

"I love these berries. You have to try them," he said as he handed Isla a couple. Isla bit into one and slowly chewed. The taste was amazing. It was almost like the berry was filled with sherbet.

As she swallowed it, she could feel the juice from inside the berry bubbling inside her tummy, but she didn't burp. She tried her hardest, but nothing was forthcoming. Oliver passed her a couple more. Again, she swallowed them and felt the bubbling sensation but still no belching. All of a sudden it came: it was like an eruption from inside her stomach. Isla let out a long and loud burp, and as she did, she flew high up into the air.

"Wooooooooooo," she cried as she flew up high into the sky and above the trees. The view above the treetops was amazing, and as she floated up in the air, she took a moment to take it all in.

As she looked back towards the hill they had come over, she could just make out something coming over the top of it. She had no idea what it was, but it looked massive and hairy and very, very scary. Before she could get a better look, she started to float back down. She kicked her legs trying to make herself get back onto the ground quicker. As she landed safely, Oliver and Fartybubble came running over to her, both laughing and smiling.

"How fun is that, let's do it again," shouted Oliver.

"But before we do, what's that coming over the hill? Is it a monster?!" Isla asked with panic in her voice.

The two boys turned around to look in the direction that Isla was pointing. Sure enough, there was a huge creature coming over the top of the hill and heading down towards the orchard. In fact, there wasn't just one of them, there was ten or twelve of these enormous beasts that Isla could see.

They were the size of elephants but very hairy, like woolly sheep ready to be sheared. A large horn stuck out from their nose, and to Isla they looked far from friendly. Their sheer size caused a large shadow to be cast over the orchard, and as they plodded down the hill, the whole ground started to rumble and vibrate.

"Elemamoths!" said Oliver, the smile now gone off his face. "We need to get out of here," and with that, he turned and ran off through the trees.

"Come on," he shouted back to Isla and Fartybubble.

As they darted off through the orchard trying to put as much distance between them and the elemamoths, their pursuers quickened their pace as well. These giant creatures went from plodding down the hill to a fast walk and then into a full on run. They covered the ground between the hill and the orchard at frightening speed.

Isla looked back over her shoulder and saw them closing the distance. How come everything can run so fast around here, she thought to herself? The elemamoths' giant feet crashing into the ground at such speed was causing the entire area to shake like they were in the middle of an earthquake. Frothing berries were falling off the trees and pelting Isla and the boys as if they were running through a fruity hailstorm. One of the berries hit Fartybubble in the centre of his forehead, exploded, and sent berry juice everywhere.

"Ahh... I'm bleeding," screamed Fartybubble as red liquid ran down his face and into his eyes

Oliver spun round to see what was happening.

"It's just berry juice," he shouted to his panicking brother.

Fartybubble wiped it out of his eyes and then licked it off his fingers just to make sure. The sweet taste of the frothing berry hit the back of his throat immediately, followed by the customary burp.

"Woooo," shouted Fartybubble as he shot up into the air

Oliver again spun round to see what his brother was doing.

"What the heck are you doing up there? We need to be running away from elemamoths. Stop messing around!"

"I can't really help it!" came the cry from high above.

"Come on, they are getting closer. Get down from there," Isla screamed at Fartybubble as the elemamoths reached the edge of the orchard.

Fartybubble floated back down to the ground and into his brother's arms. Oliver didn't hang around. He raced off, dragging his older brother behind him.

All of a sudden, the rumbling stopped. No more berries fell from the trees and the sound of galloping elemamoths ceased.

"Wait," shouted Isla, she had come to a stop and was staring back towards the elemamoths. "Look at that," she said, pointing in the direction of the orchard.

Oliver and Fartybubble came to a stop just ahead and turned around to see what Isla was looking at. The giant creatures that had seemingly been chasing them had come to a stop in the orchard and were now happily eating the frothing berries.

"They just wanted the berries," Isla said with a sigh of relief.

"I knew that," said Oliver with a grin. "Elemamoths are fruit eaters only. I remember learning that in forest school."

"So, why did you run?" asked Isla.

Before Oliver had chance to answer, there was a loud sound like a thunderclap that made all the trees shake again followed by the sight of an elemamoth flying up into the air.

"Wow," cried Isla, Oliver, and Fartybubble in unison.

"Elemamoths can burp. Well, I didn't learn that in forest school," said Oliver.

The three of them watched on as elemamoth after elemamoth shot up into the air like giant jack-in-the-boxes. The sight of these huge animals flying up into the sky was hilarious and before long the trio were on the floor laughing hysterically.

Isla held her sides; they actually ached from laughing so hard. For a few moments, she had forgotten about trying to get back home to her family and the quest she was currently on. She stood back up and composed herself, trying her hardest to ignore the elemamoths that were still shooting up into the air like giant woolly fireworks.

"So, what's the next item we need to get?" she asked, looking over to Oliver. He picked himself off the ground and dusted himself down.

"You do still have the map?" Isla asked, remembering what happened last time Oliver was in charge of one.

"Of course, I have," he said, pulling the map out of the waistband of his trousers and holding it up proudly.

He unfolded the map and studied it before declaring, "The next item is the buzzagon feather which is that way," he said pointing the way they had been running which luckily was the opposite direction to the elemamoths.

"Is this when you tell us that buzzagons only eat fruit as well?" Isla asked rather hopefully.

Oliver just laughed and shook his head. Fartybubble, on the other hand, looked worried at the thought of where they were heading next.

"Don't worry, it will be fine. We probably won't even see a buzzagon. All we need to do is head towards their nest, and I'm sure we will find a few feathers lying around that they have shed while flying. We only have two more items to get. Come on, bro, we will be home in no time," Oliver said, sounding highly confident.

Fartybubble mumbled something under his breath about buzzagons and goblins, but Oliver either didn't hear it or just chose to ignore it.

"But before we go, one last thing," said Oliver.

"What's that?" asked Isla.

"This," and with that, Oliver pulled out a couple of berries he had stashed in his pocket and popped them into his mouth. One massive burp later and he was flying high into the sky, laughing all the way. Fartybubble just shook his head and tutted, but Isla couldn't help but smile. She had always dreamt of adventures in far off lands and at this moment in time she was actually in one for real, and she was starting to enjoy herself. Whether that enjoyment would last, though, time would tell.

Chapter 6

After the trio had left the orchard, the map took them down into a valley and led them along a path next to a stream. The water that flowed through the valley was crystal clear and looked good enough to drink. As they walked, Oliver stopped, and he dropped onto his knees and scooped some water into his hands and took a big gulp of it, letting out a large sigh as he did so.

"Ah, refreshing," he said.

Isla looked on. Her mouth felt dry, and she was very thirsty, but she was unsure about drinking from a stream. Oliver looked over his shoulder and saw Isla watching him. He motioned to her to come and join him by the stream.

"Come and get a drink. The water is lovely here," Oliver said.

"Is it safe?" Isla asked.

"Of course, it is. This is the same stream that flows all the way into the forest and near our village. Unkerdunkies have been drinking this stuff for years, and it's never done us any harm. Isn't that right, bro?" Oliver said, calling to his brother.

Isla turned around to see what Fartybubble had to say on the matter, but he was already down by the edge of the stream taking in handfuls of the tempting looking water. This made up Isla's mind, so, she went over and knelt by the side of Oliver and took a big gulp of the refreshing looking liquid.

"Umm," Isla said as she took gulp after gulp. The water tasted amazing here and reminded her of the posh bottled water with the strange name that her dad sometimes bought before her mum would moan about how expensive it was.

After taking plenty of water on board, the three of them continued on their way. Isla felt energised and full of beans. She wasn't sure what was in the water, but she felt ready to take on the world.

After following the stream a short while longer, the map indicated that they must cross it and take a path that led up to the top of the valley. Oliver was the first one across, hopping over the stream and landing safely on the other side. He turned around and held his hand out to Isla, although she didn't really need his help. The stream wasn't that wide, and with her longer legs than the little Unkerdunkie, she could easily stride across it; nonetheless, she accepted his help and thanked him.

Once Fartybubble was safely across as well, Oliver led the way up the fairly steep path that wound its way up the side of the valley. The going was pretty tough as the path was starting to wear away in places, and the three of them moved slowly as so not to lose their footing.

Once Oliver had safely made it to the top, he stood with his hands on his hips and looked out into the distance.

"Buzzagon land," he said, mainly to himself.

Isla followed closely behind and joined Oliver by his side and took in the sight in front of her.

"IT'S SNOWING," she exclaimed.

The picture in front of her was very different to what she had literally just left behind. Everything was white, the sky was grey, and flakes of snow floated down onto the ground.

"Of course, it's snowing, the buzzagons are warm blooded animals and like the snow. That is why they live here."

Isla turned around and looked back into the valley at where she had just come from: the lush green grass and the blue skies and bright sunshine with still not a cloud to be seen.

"But it's sunny there and now this. How can that be?" she asked, feeling a little confused at what she was seeing.

"Because this part of Atalan is known as Snowy Point, and the weather is like this all the time. The place we have just come from is known as Forest Glades. There, it is sunny and warm all the time. That's why we live there. Unkerdunkies love the sunshine, and the trees need the sunlight and the warmth to grow," said Oliver.

"But doesn't it ever rain in the forest? Surely the trees need water as well as sunlight to grow?" asked Isla. She wasn't an expert in trees and plants, but she had listened in school and knew how things grew.

"Not the trees in Forest Glades. Water would make them shrivel up and die. When we go to the Goblin Kingdom, then you will see very different types of trees and plants because there it rains all the time. For some reason, goblins love the wet," Oliver said, shrugging his shoulders as to why anyone would enjoy the rain. Oliver looked at Isla who still seemed confused by the sudden change in weather conditions.

"Isn't it like this on Earth? Don't you have different weather zones?" Oliver asked.

"No, we have seasons. So, in summer it's usually sunny and warm, and then in winter it's often cold and snowy. You wouldn't just step out of one place where it is bright sunshine and straight into a place that's covered in snow."

"What a strange place you live," said Oliver, scratching his head. Just then, Fartybubble reached the top and came and stood by the side of his brother. He looked out across the snowy landscape before him.

"So, where exactly is the map taking us?" he asked his brother.

"That way," Oliver said, pointing across the snowy ground in front of them and towards a range of snow-capped hills in the distance.

"Oh, great, so we need to climb a mountain to get to the buzzagons," said Fartybubble with a large sigh.

"It's more of a hill than a mountain," replied Oliver.

"Oh, and what's the difference?" asked Fartybubble in a slightly sarcastic tone.

"Hills are easier to climb than mountains; they are less steep and not as high. A hill becomes a mountain at 2000ft or 609.6m or over," answered Oliver with a smile on his face.

Both Isla and Fartybubble looked at him in surprise.

"What?" said Oliver "I listen in forest school."

And with that, he set off towards the hill, calling to his companions as he went.

"Keep an eye out for feathers on the ground. We might find them before we even reach the hills. Oh, and don't eat yellow snow," he said, laughing.

Isla followed Oliver, her feet crunching through the snow as she walked. It was hard going as it was fairly deep in places, and at times, the snow would come over the top of her trainers. Isla really wasn't dressed for the snow, she thought to herself, dressed only in jeans, trainers and a thin sweatshirt.

101

Normally, if she was to go out in the snow, she would be wearing a hat, scarf, gloves, and a big coat. She hated being cold, especially her fingers and ears, but as she trudged through the snow, she realised something. She wasn't cold at all; the temperature didn't feel any different to when they had been in the forest and the sun had been beating down on them. Even though all around her was snow and the sky was overcast and grey, she didn't feel cold in the slightest.

Isla bent down and scooped up a handful of snow and moulded it into a ball. To her complete surprise, the snow was warm to touch. It felt more like warm sand in her hands rather than freezing snow as she expected. But here in her hand was a warm compact snowball that wasn't melting. It was crazy and was starting to mess with her head.

First stepping out of a forest where it was sunny and bright straight into deep snow and grey skies, then being told about the different weather zones, and now holding a warm snowball in her hand. Atalan certainly was another world, she thought to herself, and full of surprises.

As she stood there with the snowball warming her hands, she looked over towards Oliver further ahead. He was walking with his head down scanning the floor for feathers as he went. Isla looked at the nice sized snowball in her hand and then back over towards Oliver and then back to the snowball.

The temptation to throw it was very high, but she decided against it. They were here to find the items needed to help her get home and not mess about. Oliver and Fartybubble were kindly helping her in this task, and neither of them needed pelting with a snowball. Isla threw the snowball onto the ground and brushed her hands together before continuing on her way.

She had only taken a couple of steps when smack, she felt something hit her on the back of her head. She spun round to see Fartybubble standing not far behind her with a big grin on his face. He was already bending down and moulding another snowball ready to launch her way.

"Oh, like that is it," laughed Isla.

She bent down and started making a snowball of her own as quickly as possible whilst trying to keep an eye on Fartybubble. As she was in the process of moulding her own snowball, one came flying towards her. Isla instinctively dodged to her right, and the snowball whistled over her left shoulder. Before Fartybubble could scoop up any more snow, Isla had taken a giant swing with her right arm and sent her snowball flying towards her target.

"Yes," Isla shouted out in delight as her snowball crashed into Fartybubble, hitting him on his head and exploding into flakes. The impact of the snowball took his hat clean off and knocked the little Unkerdunkie off his feet. He landed on his back in a way it looked like he was trying to create a snow angel. At the sight of this, Isla burst out laughing, but after a couple of seconds, she stopped as Fartybubble hadn't got up. She hoped she hadn't hurt him or upset him. She was only having a bit of fun, and after all, it was he who had started it. She walked towards her prone opponent to check he was ok, but as she got closer, he sat up and in one swift movement had thrown a snowball into her face!

"Haha, I got you," laughed Fartybubble, obviously ecstatic that his trick had worked. With that, the two of them started launching snowball after snowball towards each other while all the time laughing out loud.

Oliver, who was further ahead, stopped in his tracks and turned around to see what all the commotion was. He was shocked to see his older, and normally more sensible, brother engaged in a snowball fight with Isla.

"Hey, I thought we were meant to be finding feathers, not messing around," he called as he started walking back towards the snowballing pair.

"Although it does look fun," he said mainly to himself. And with that, he made himself a snowball and ran over to join in with the ongoing battle. For the next few minutes, the air was filled with the sound of laughter and shouting as the trio pelted each other with warm soft snow. Eventually, after much running, throwing, ducking and dodging, all three of them fell to the ground in a tired heap.

"That's the most fun I've had in ages," panted Fartybubble as he wiped snow off his tunic.

"It's great to have a snowball fight and not be freezing cold by the end of it or have numb fingers," laughed Isla.

"Why would you be freezing or have numb fingers from a snowball fight?" enquired Oliver.

"Doesn't matter," answered Isla, she didn't want to confuse Oliver by explaining how on Earth snow was cold.

"Shall we get back to trying to find buzzagon feathers?" she said as she stood up and brushed the snow off herself.

Oliver nodded his agreement. He stood up and retrieved the map which he had once more placed within the safety of his waistband and set off again following the arrow towards the hills. Isla followed closely behind with Fartybubble again bringing up the rear. He was still chuckling to himself as they walked.

All three of them scanned the floor as they went in the hope they would spot a couple of feathers before they had to tackle the hill. Isla didn't really know what she was looking for but guessed feathers from a large beast that resembled a dragon would be pretty distinctive and would certainly stand out amongst the whiteness that surrounded them. Unfortunately, they saw nothing apart from snow and eventually they reached the bottom of a steep hill or possibly mountain which the map indicated they must climb.

There was what appeared to be a path that seemed to lead all the way up to the top of the hill that the trio could follow. Unfortunately, the path was covered in ice rather than the thick, soft snow that they had previously been walking through. The ice glistened in front of them like a shiny mirror. Isla didn't fancy their chances of making it up the path in a hurry, if at all. Maybe though, ice in Atalan wasn't slippery at all, thought Isla. After all, snow was warm, so, maybe the path would be easy to climb. Looking at the hill, there certainly seemed no other way of getting to the top. Either side of the icy path the hill was covered in bushes, rocks, and trees, all covered in thick snow. There seemed no way through all of that, so the path looked like the only option.

"So, we have to get to the top of this mountain?" asked Fartybubble as he stood at the bottom of the path and gazed up to the summit.

"Hill," replied Oliver, correcting his brother. "Yes, the map is pointing up to the top. Come on. It shouldn't take us long," with that, Oliver took a couple of steps up the path before sliding back down to where he started. Ice obviously was slippery in Atalan, Isla thought.

"Why don't we fly up?" said Fartybubble.

"Well, we only have a limited amount of the potion, and I think we are better waiting until we really need it. I think it will be more useful when we get to the Goblin Kingdom. What do you think, Isla?" Oliver asked.

Isla took another look at the hill in front of her. It was certainly steep and by the looks of it, very slippery all the way to the top. It would be so much easier just to fly up to the summit, but Oliver had a point. If they could somehow get up to the top without using the limited amount of potion they had and save it for later, then that would be better.

"Why don't we attempt to climb the path? If we can't do it, then we will have to use the flying potion," said Isla

"Good idea," said Oliver, and with that, he started climbing the path again. This time, he made it a bit further before slipping. Isla and Fartybubble followed after him but didn't fare much better. It felt like trying to walk on an ice rink, Isla thought. It was one step forward and then two steps slipping back. This was going to take all day at this rate; maybe flying was the answer, thought Isla.

As she slipped back down the hill for what felt like the hundredth time, she suddenly had an idea. Amongst the trees and bushes that lined the path were many twigs and branches that had fallen to the ground. Isla managed to grab a couple and started using them as makeshift walking poles. She would push them into the ground and break the ice finding the slightly firmer ground below and pull herself up. She knew that the time she had spent one

107

evening watching a documentary with her dad about a group of celebrities who had climbed Mount Everest would come in handy one day.

"Grab yourself some sticks, and do what I'm doing," shouted Isla as she started making progress up the hill.

Oliver and Fartybubble looked up from their positions towards the bottom of the hill and watched in amazement as Isla started to disappear up the path. They quickly found suitable sticks within the undergrowth and followed quite literally in Isla's footsteps. It was still hard going, and at times the sticks would slip from underneath them, and they would slide back slightly or end up flat on their faces. But the trio were making progress, and the summit was starting to get closer.

Eventually, Isla made it to the top. She fell to the ground exhausted, her arms and legs burning from the effort. As she lay on the ground trying to catch her breath, she remembered what was meant to be at the top of this hill: a giant fire breathing creature that wasn't a dragon but pretty much was!

She shot up off the ground and quickly surveyed her surroundings, making sure she wasn't lying next to a sleeping buzzagon. Luckily, there wasn't a buzzagon to be seen. In fact, there wasn't that much at all at the top of the hill except for a few trees dotted around, a couple of large rocks, and something on the far side of the hill that resembled a giant bird's nest.

As Isla took in her surroundings, she was joined by Oliver and Fartybubble who appeared at the top of the hill puffing and panting. They collapsed on the floor next to her, exhausted from the effort of the climb.

"Are you two ok?" asked Isla.

Oliver flashed her a grin and nodded whilst Fartybubble's only response was a grunt. Oliver pulled himself to his feet and examined the map. The arrow was pointing directly to this spot. They had reached the location of the feathers they needed.

"They must be around there," said Oliver pointing towards the structure Isla had spotted. "That must be a buzzagon's nest."

As Isla took a closer look at the nest, which was made out of a combination of twigs and leaves, she could see something inside was moving. It wasn't very big, whatever it was, maybe the size of a small bird. As she continued to watch, heads starting popping up and appearing above the nest. She counted maybe seven or eight of these tiny creatures. They may have been bird sized but they looked very different from the feathered variety she knew. They looked more like the lizards Isla had seen during a recent school trip to the zoo, although these ones had wings.

"Shouldn't we use the invisibility potion if we are this close to a buzzagon's nest?" asked Fartybubble nervously.

"Why waste it? If there were any adult buzzagons around we would have known about it by now. They are just chicks in the nest, and they can't harm us. They don't start flying until they are two and won't start breathing fire until much later," Oliver said with a smile.

Fartybubble gave his brother yet another look of surprise at his knowledge.

"Did you learn that in forest school as well? How come I haven't learnt any of this stuff?"

"No, I read it in the book Wally showed us. Anyway, I can creep over to the nest, grab a couple of feathers, and we can be on our way before the buzzagons get back. There's plenty lying around," Oliver said, pointing towards the nest.

Oliver was indeed right, Isla noticed. All around the nest lay feathers of different sizes. At first, Isla had thought the green objects lying in the snow were leaves that had fallen from the trees, but on closer inspection, she could make out they were indeed feathers which had most likely been shed by the adult buzzagons during take-off and landing.

Oliver set off towards the nest, moving as carefully as possible, trying not to slip or make too much noise and frighten the young chicks.

As he walked, the ice crunched and cracked below him, and with each sound, Fartybubble would whisper "sshh" which Isla didn't think was really helping! Oliver got within a few metres from the nest and stopped. He carefully bent down and

110

picked up two of the larger feathers and carefully placed them into his pocket. As he stood back up, the ice below him once again cracked. This time the sound was met by a chorus of squawking and chirping coming from the nest.

Oliver headed back towards Isla and Fartybubble, moving as quickly as he could without losing his footing. Suddenly, the noise of the chicks was drowned out by a terrifying roar so loud that it made the trees shake and the snow fall from the branches.

"What was that?!" shouted Isla, trying to make herself heard above the roar.

"That," screamed Fartybubble, pointing into the sky.

Through the grey skies came an object that was the size of a small plane with huge wings. Unlike a plane, though, this was covered in bright green feathers, had razor-sharp claws, fang-like teeth and was spitting fire. It was also travelling through the air at a vast rate and was heading straight towards the trio.

"BUZZAGON!" shouted Oliver. "Take cover!" he said as he made a dash for a nearby tree.

He skidded across the ice and ended up in a heap in a pile of softer snow at the bottom of the tree trunk. Isla looked around to see what there was to take cover behind. The closest thing to her and Fartybubble was a large rock that was protruding out the ground. Isla grabbed Fartybubble's arm and pulled him towards the rock.

As she moved, her feet gave way on the ice, and she went flying. As she fell, she felt something snap. Luckily, it wasn't a bone but instead the strap that had been holding the bag in place had broken.

Isla and Fartybubble both fell into a heap behind the rock, and Isla immediately realised that the bag had come loose and was no longer safely tucked under her right arm. As she frantically looked around for the missing bag, the buzzagon swooped down towards the hilltop and let out another ear-splitting roar, but this time it was accompanied by a ferocious fireball that shot through the air towards the tree that Oliver was currently hiding behind.

The flames crackled through the air setting fire to the branches of the tree. There was a whoosh of steam as the flames met the snow-covered branches causing a deluge of water to fall onto Oliver below as the snow above him melted.

"Woo," he screamed as the water hit him and soaked him from head to toe.

The flames took hold of the tree in seconds, and the air was filled with the sounds of creaking and cracking. One huge branch snapped off the tree and fell to the ground narrowly missing Oliver. The branch hit the floor with a bang and then slipped along the icy ground and came to a rest at the edge of the hill, teetering over the top of the path that the trio had only recently climbed. The buzzagon rolled away to its right before banking back round, ready to launch another attack.

"Maybe now is a good time to use the invisibility potion?!" screamed Fartybubble.

"Only one slight problem with that idea," said Isla pointing over to where the bag now rested. It was lying on the floor right next to the fallen branch.

"We need to make a run for it," shouted a soaked Oliver from behind the tree that was still standing but now on fire. "Quickly, before the buzzagon attacks again. If it lands, we are in big trouble."

Isla had her eyes fixed on the bag. Could she make a run for it and grab the invisibility potion before the buzzagon struck again? It was already heading back towards the hilltop and moving at an alarming pace. The bag was only a few metres in front of her, lying on the ice next to the branch that was perched precariously on top of the hill like a toboggan at the top of a run.

"The branch looks like a toboggan," Isla said out loud to herself.

"WHAT?!" shouted Fartybubble. He had no idea what she was going on about.

Isla looked at the branch. It was big, certainly big enough for the three of them to sit on it, and it was resting right on the edge of the hill, a very slippery hill. One little nudge and it would go flying down there like a sledge.

"I have an idea. Get to the branch and sit on it. We are going to slide down the hill," Isla shouted. She had no idea if it would work, but it was worth a shot. She had slid down hills with her dad on a tin tray before so why not a large branch.

Oliver didn't need telling twice, mainly because the tree he was hiding behind was now a raging inferno and likely to fall down any minute either crushing him or leaving him a sitting duck for the buzzagon. He got up and skidded across the ice like an out of control figure skater towards the branch. Once he had reached it, he threw himself on top of it. The ice underneath cracked, and the branch wobbled. For a second, Isla thought it was going to disappear over the edge and carry Oliver away.

"Come on, we need to go NOW," Isla shouted at Fartybubble who was still cowering behind the rock. She grabbed his arm and hoisted him up and onto his feet before giving him a gentle nudge towards his brother. He skidded across the ice and fell onto the branch just behind Oliver. Isla skidded over the ice to join them. She grabbed the bag off the ground as she passed it and stuffed it inside her sweatshirt for safety. By now, the buzzagon had them in its sights and was swooping in for a second attack.

"HOLD ON TIGHT," Isla shouted at the top of her voice.

"HOLD ONTO WHAT?!" shouted Fartybubble.

"ANYTHING!" screamed Isla, and as she did, she gave the branch a push and then jumped onto the back. She grabbed hold of Fartybubble who was gripping the branch with all his might while Oliver hung onto a smaller branch that was sticking out the front. The branch wobbled at first and then disappeared over the top of the hill and started to slide, slowly at first, but then it gradually started to pick up speed.

"COME ON, COME ON, FASTER," screamed Isla as she looked back over her shoulder and could see the buzzagon approaching fast, its giant wings flapping vigorously and its mouth wide open ready to unleash another fireball.

"Woo," screamed Oliver, who was obviously enjoying the ride and had completely forgotten about the fire breathing beast that was right behind them.

All of a sudden, the branch really started to slide. It flew down the hill completely out of control! Just as it picked up pace, the buzzagon roared again and sent another fireball soaring towards the escaping trio.

"HOW DO YOU STOP THIS THING?!" Fartybubble screamed.

"YOU CAN'T," shouted Isla. "AND YOU REALLY WOULDN'T WANT IT TO STOP RIGHT NOW!"

The flames were getting closer and closer and were melting the ice. It was starting to become less like a toboggan run and more like a waterslide. Isla looked forward. They were quickly running out of hill, and the buzzagon wasn't giving up. The flames kept coming, like one continuous stream of fire that at any second would engulf the branch. Isla put her head down and closed her eyes tightly. She could feel the heat on her back. All she could think of was her loving family back home and how she would never see them again. She held her breath and waited for the flame to hit the bark.

"WOOOOO," screamed Oliver as the branch hit a bump in the ground which launched it into the air just as the flames hit the spot where a moment ago the branch had been. Isla dared to open her eyes for a second. The ice below was fast approaching as the branch plummeted towards the ground. She held onto Fartybubble as tightly as she could while he dug his fingers so hard into the branch that they were starting to turn white.

Oliver, meanwhile, had one hand on the small branch and his other arm in the air like he was a cowboy at a rodeo riding a bull! The branch crashed back down onto the hill with a thud and just ahead of the incoming fire. The buzzagon gave one last blast of flames and then barrelled away and

116

back towards the hilltop and its chicks, happy that it had seen off the danger to its babies. The branch came soaring off the bottom of the hill, slid across the ice, and smashed into a pile of deep soft snow, sending its passengers flying.

Isla lay still not daring to move. She was completely covered by the snow, and she was afraid that if she popped her head out, she would see the buzzagon angrily hovering above ready to finish them off.

"What a rush!" It was Oliver's voice that broke the silence as he popped up from out the snow. Isla slowly raised her head above the snowdrift and scanned the sky above. There was no sign of the buzzagon. It must have flown back to the nest, she thought. With the coast being clear, Isla slowly pulled herself out of the mound of snow that had cushioned her landing and checked to make sure nothing was broken and that she still had the bag safely stashed inside her top.

"That was awesome," shouted Oliver. "And I didn't drop these," he said excitedly as he pulled the two feathers from his snow-filled pocket.

As Oliver stood there, waving the feathers around like he was doing some kind of Morris dance, Fartybubble's head appeared out of the snow. It reminded Isla of the game she used to play at the amusement arcades where you had to whack a mole with a hammer, and for some reason it made her laugh. Maybe it was more down to the relief of surviving the buzzagon and the joy of getting the feathers rather than the sight of Fartybubble's head sticking out the snow that made her laugh uncontrollably, but whatever it was, she couldn't stop. As she laughed, it made Oliver laugh as well and soon both of them had tears streaming down their cheeks. Fartybubble just stared at them from the snow.

"What's so funny?" he asked.

"I've no idea," laughed Oliver.

Eventually, the pair of them calmed down and pulled Fartybubble out of the snowdrift and helped brush him down. Oliver handed Isla the feathers which she stored into the strapless bag before safely putting it back inside her top. Oliver opened the map and checked to see which way the arrow was now sending them.

"Only one more item left to find," said Oliver "Goblin Kingdom here we come."

Chapter 7

The map safely led the three adventurers around the bottom of the hill and away from the angry buzzagon. Luckily, there were no more sightings of any fire breathing winged creatures, and the only sign of them being around was the occasional loud roar in the distance which made Fartybubble jump every time.

After leaving the hill behind them, the landscape once again changed. The deep soft snow was replaced with more solid ground made up of patches of grass and dried mud.

This sudden change once again astounded Isla. One second her feet were covered in thick snow and then the next step forward, and she was standing on slightly damp grass. It was as if two photographs had been joined together, showing completely different environments. The grey skies and snowy landscape that were now behind her had been replaced with a more foreboding scene. In front of her was the kind of setting she would expect to see in a scary movie or a book about a haunted wood and witches.

The sky was very dark and filled with large, black clouds looking ready to unleash a torrent of rain and thunder. The grass wasn't the bright, lush green colour of Forest Glade, but instead, it was brown and patchy; in many places, it was more mud than grass. The few trees that were dotted around had hardly any leaves on them and the ones they had looked dead, wilting and brown in colour. A strong wind whipped up the leaves from the ground and eerily whistled all around them, at times sounding like a voice in the distance daring you to come forward. It was the type of place you would do your best to avoid, and yet the arrow on the map was pointing directly towards it.

"So, it looks like we need to head that way," said Oliver, pointing beyond some trees slightly to the left of where they stood. He didn't seem phased by the thought of walking through this part of Atalan, Isla thought, but then, he didn't seem to be phased by much at all!

"Beyond the trees, it looks like there is a river and a bridge that we have to cross. Over the other side is Goblin Kingdom," said Oliver, closely examining the map.

"A bridge?" said Fartybubble, looking over to his younger brother. "You don't mean...?"

"I don't know if it's that bridge. The map just shows a bridge," Oliver replied.

"Which bridge, what are you two on about?" asked Isla who was slightly confused.

"There is a story that is told about an uncrossable bridge that leads to Goblin Kingdom," replied Oliver.

"Why is it uncrossable?" asked Isla.

"Because a giant troll lives underneath the bridge who throws anyone who tries to cross into the river below," answered Fartybubble with a look of dread on his face.

"A troll under a bridge. Do you mean like in the three billy goats gruff?" asked Isla.

"What on Atalan is that?" asked Fartybubble.

"It's a fairy tale about a troll who lives under a bridge and three pigs who want to get across," replied Isla.

"A fairies tale? What have fairies got to do with all this?" asked a puzzled Oliver.

"Not a fairies tale, a fairy tale. It is a story that adults tell their children often before bed," replied Isla.

"And is it true?" asked Fartybubble.

"No, not at all. Fairy tales are just made up," answered Isla with a smile. She hoped that trolls were also something that were made up here on Atalan as well.

"You see," said Oliver looking towards his brother, "it's a made up story back on Earth as well. It is probably something the elders tell us just to put anyone off from trying to get into Goblin Kingdom. Plus, we don't even know if this is the same bridge. This is a magic map, remember. It might be showing us the safest path across. This may be a crossable bridge for all we know."

"I don't need a story about an uncrossable bridge to stop me wanting to go to Goblin

Kingdom. The fact that there are goblins there is enough to put me off," said Fartybubble, who once again looked rather worried.

"Why are goblins so bad?" asked Isla. She had watched many an animated film that had featured goblins and every time they were portrayed as being the villain.

"Goblins are a fighting race, that's what they do. They drink their brew, sing and dance, drink more brew and then fight. Usually just with each other, but they have been known to attack other races," replied Oliver.

"Have they ever attacked the Unkerdunkies?" asked Isla, hoping that the answer would be no but guessing it probably wouldn't be.

"According to stories, a very long time ago an army of goblins left their kingdom and travelled across Atalan to the Forest Glades. They came to take over our villages and make the Unkerdunkies their slaves," answered Fartybubble.

"What happened?" asked Isla.

"Well," said Oliver, picking up the story, "legend has it that while the goblins are feared fighters, they are not the smartest. Also, a weakness of theirs is that they cannot climb trees. When they arrived in the forest, the Unkerdunkies simply retreated into their villages, and then, from the safety of the higher positions in the trees, they attacked the goblins with whatever they could lay their hands on."

"Yeah, the goblins were pelted with berries, sticks, shoes, buckets, whatever was available. The goblins were driven out of the forest and back to their kingdom," continued Fartybubble with a smile.

"Story goes that on their retreat back to Goblin Kingdom, the army was attacked by a flock of angry buzzagons that chased them all the way back to their kingdom. Since then, they have never left there again," added Oliver, looking very proud of his brave ancestors.

"So, as you can imagine, we won't be very welcome within their kingdom, especially when we are trying to steal from them," said a very nervous looking Fartybubble.

"Everything will be fine, trust me. We will get across the bridge, drink the invisibility potion, grab a bottle of brew without the goblins knowing, and then fly away to safety. It will be as easy as that. What could possibly go wrong?" replied a confident sounding Oliver.

It certainly sounded straightforward enough, thought Isla, even if the look on Fartybubble's face suggested otherwise.

"Come on, let's follow the map and find this bridge," said Oliver as he marched off towards the trees in the distance with Isla and Fartybubble following behind.

As they walked, the rain started to fall, lightly at first, but it wasn't long before the dark clouds above started to rumble and erupt into a heavy downpour, soaking the trio below within seconds. Where the snow had been surprisingly warm, the rain in Atalan certainly wasn't. The huge drops that fell at such a rate were ice cold, and it wasn't long before Isla was shivering from the torrent; her clothes literally clinging to her body and feeling twice as heavy. The trees offered little cover due to the distinct lack of leaves on the branches, and there seemed no let up from this weather.

Isla remembered Oliver saying how the goblins loved the rain and being wet and since you only seemed to get one type of weather condition at each place you went, it looked like the rain was going to keep falling until they left Goblin Kingdom.

Isla pulled her sleeves down as far as they went in an attempt to keep her fingers warm and tucked her chin down to her chest. She could feel the water squelching inside her trainers as the ground turned boggy and the rain found a way inside her footwear. White trainers were certainly not the best type of footwear for this environment, Isla thought, as she kept trudging forwards.

As she walked, she noticed it was starting to become misty. The further they went, the thicker the mist got, really adding to the already eerie surroundings, thought Isla. Through the mist, Isla could make out some trees ahead that seemed to offer a little bit of shelter from the elements due to the denser cover they provided. The branches were covered in what looked like thick black leaves that swayed in the wind. The way they moved it was almost as if they were alive. As Isla got within a few metres of these trees, their leaves suddenly sprouted wings, and within an instant, the sky was filled with hundreds of flying black creatures that let out an ear-splitting clicking noise.

"Bats," screamed Isla dropping to the floor as the beasts flew over her head. They were so close she could feel the draft their flapping wings were creating.

"Daggermoths," screamed Fartybubble, also dropping to the floor in panic.

"They won't hurt you," said Oliver calmly, as the creatures soared up into the sky.

"Are you sure?" said Isla, looking up from the ground.

"Of course. Daggermoths eat nothing more than berries and small grubs. They are far more scared of us than we are of them," said Oliver, looking down at his two prone companions. "Well, normally," he added.

Isla picked herself off the sodden ground and looked up at the mass of daggermoths that had filled the sky above her. They certainly looked like bats from here, she thought, with their black bodies and large black wings.

"I thought you would have known daggermoths were harmless, bro, don't you listen to anything Elder Attenborough tells us at forest school?" Oliver asked his brother.

"You know woodland studies isn't my favourite subject. I much prefer art and poetry," replied Fartybubble.

"If they are harmless, then why have they got the word dagger in their name? It doesn't sound very harmless to me," asked Isla.

"It's because of the way they pick up berries and grubs. They spear them with their claws like a dagger and then carry the food back to their nests before eating it," said Oliver with a smile. He obviously enjoyed being able to give facts out about the many weird and wonderful creatures that inhabited Atalan.

"Oh, I see," Isla said as she watched the mass of black disappear off into the distance, probably looking for some more trees to hang off away from the three people who had rudely disturbed them.

"Fun fact for you, the goblins consider daggermoths a delicacy. Although, to be honest, goblins will eat most things. Anyway, according to the map, we are not too far from the bridge. Follow me," and once again Oliver set off leading the way through the now bare trees.

As they walked through the mist and the rain, Isla could hear something up ahead, a faint sound at first that gradually got louder and louder. It was the sound of running water. It must be the river, thought Isla, and it sounded fierce.

"There," shouted Oliver from the front of the group. He was pointing to a bridge that was just up ahead. The three of them slowly approached the riverbank and the edge of the bridge. Through the mist, Isla could make out the water below. It was a fair drop down to the water, but even from here, she could tell that it wasn't the kind of river you would want to fall into. The water was dark and uninviting. It was flowing very fast, crashing over rocks that stuck out from the riverbed and carrying debris with it from small twigs and sticks to large branches and even whole trees.

"Is this the uncrossable bridge?" asked Fartybubble.

"I don't know. It looks pretty crossable to me, and anyway, I don't see another way to get over the river," answered Oliver.

Isla scanned the riverbank. Oliver was right. There didn't seem to be any other way across except for this bridge in front of them. It certainly looked safe and stable enough, certainly for the weight of two Unkerdunkies and a ten year old girl, she thought, and there was no sign of any mythical troll lurking anywhere nearby ready to jump out.

The bridge itself was made of wooden planks with small gaps in between each one in which you could see down to the murky water below. On each side of the bridge, there was a guide rope that you could hold onto that ran the entire length of the structure. The bridge was fairly long; Isla estimated that it was at least half the length of her school's running track, and it was wide enough for two people to cross side by side.

"Why don't we use the invisibility potion now? Then even if there is a troll, it wouldn't see us crossing the bridge," said Fartybubble, who was obviously worrying once again.

"There is no point in wasting it. We will need to use it to get past the goblins. Look, there are no trolls around, and this bridge looks perfectly safe. Even Isla said that trolls are something made up back on Earth as well," said Oliver, trying to put his brother's mind at rest.

"We could even fly across," said Fartybubble.

As the two Unkerdunkies continued to bicker about the best way of getting across the river, Isla stepped forward and placed her right foot onto the first plank of the bridge. It creaked slightly but took her weight. She was cold and soaking wet and didn't want to stand around for any longer listening to these two argue. They only had one more item to get to make the potion that would hopefully get her back home to her family and that item was just across this bridge. She wasn't waiting.

"Right, I'm going for it," she said.

"Yes," shouted Oliver, punching the air with his fist.

Isla slowly started moving across the bridge. Part of her wanted to run as fast as possible to the other side, but she moved cautiously not wanting to lose her footing and fall into the dark depths of the river below. As she moved, she kept her head up and her eyes looking forward. She didn't want to look down through the gaps and see the water underneath her. Each plank creaked as she placed her foot gently onto it, and she could feel the bridge sway slightly with every step, but it felt safe enough to keep going. After she had covered six or seven planks, she heard a loud creak and the whole bridge seemed to shudder. She span around and saw Oliver had stepped onto the bridge.

"WAIT," shouted Isla.

Oliver looked up and froze.

Isla held her breath but nothing else happened.

"I'm not sure how much weight this bridge can take. Maybe we should go across one at a time to be safe," Isla called to Oliver. He nodded and very carefully and slowly retreated back off the bridge and re-joined his brother.

Isla took a moment to calm herself down and stop her legs from shaking before continuing on her way. The next couple of steps brought the usual creaking from the wooden planks but nothing else, and soon she was over halfway and feeling confident about the crossing. As she took her next step, a different sound filled the air: the splashing of water followed by a loud huffing and puffing as if someone or something was exerting themselves and attempting to climb onto the bridge.

As Isla looked straight ahead, a huge hand appeared over the guide rope on her right hand side towards the end of the bridge and the opposite riverbank. In a flash, the hand was followed by the rest of the body as a mysterious beast came bounding over the ropes and landed on the bridge. Isla braced herself and grabbed both of the guide ropes ready for the bridge to collapse.

Whatever was in front of her was massive and surely weighed a ton, and there was no way this creaking wooden bridge could possibly hold its weight. Any second, Isla thought she would be plummeting down to the river below. She closed her eyes and waited for the inevitable to happen. But the bridge didn't collapse, it hardly even shook. The beast landing on it made less impact than when Oliver had stepped foot onto it.

"TROLL," screamed Oliver and Fartybubble at the same time.

Isla spun round to see the two Unkerdunkies frantically gesturing for her to get off the bridge and back to them. But she couldn't move. It was as if she had been frozen to the spot. Her legs were shaking that much. She thought that at any second they would give way and she would collapse in a heap on the ground.

She thought about grabbing the bag that was still safely stashed inside her sweatshirt and drinking the flying potion and simply flying off the bridge to safety, but her hands were so cold she didn't know if she would even be able to undo the bottle top. Plus, her top was so wet, it was clinging to her body, which would make it difficult to retrieve the bag quickly. By the time she had got it, out the troll could have got across the bridge to her.

Instead, she just stood there, staring at the troll that was blocking her path to the Goblin Kingdom. The troll that was looking back at her was nothing like how she had imagined one would look. She had pictured something small and cute with bright coloured hair that enjoyed music and dancing.

This, on the other hand, was massive and scary looking. Its hands were like shovels, its arms and shoulders like boulders. It reminded Isla of the strongmen her dad sometimes watched on tele, who would pull buses and planes and lift giant stones, although this troll was even bigger than they were. It was wearing a green chequered shirt that looked like it was too small, and it was simply bursting out of it, as it was torn in many places, buttons were missing, and the sleeves completely ripped off. Its brown trousers were the same, torn and ripped in many places as they failed to hold its monstrous legs in. The trousers stopped short of its massive calves which were like two giant diamonds strapped to the back of its shins. The troll was barefoot, and each of its feet was the size of Isla's thighs. If this troll had green skin, it would have resembled the hulk, thought Isla.

The troll didn't move. It just stared at Isla; its large brown eyes locked onto hers. Isla stared back. She could hear the Unkerdunkies behind her still screaming at her to run, to move, to do something to get off the bridge. Her natural instinct was to move, to turn and run as quickly as possible away from the danger ahead, yet something was stopping her. Maybe it was fear that had frozen her to the spot, but she didn't think so, there was something else.

Yes, this troll was massive and looked like it could crush her with its little finger, but there was something about it. It has got kind eyes, thought Isla. She remembered what her grandma used to say, "the eyes are like the windows to your soul," and that "you can tell a lot about someone from their eyes."

This huge hulking figure was staring back at Isla with the kind of eyes you would see on a puppy who wanted to play fetch. Isla wasn't going to run from this. She had done enough running away from things today. She was going to stand her ground. She took a couple of deep breaths and composed herself before holding out her hand.

"Hello, I'm Isla, pleased to meet you."

Oliver and Fartybubble both gasped with a mixture of amazement and fear, mainly fear for Fartybubble, as they watched on from the edge of the bridge. They had both crouched down in an attempt to make themselves as small as possible, which for an Unkerdunkie was pretty easy to do, and out of sight of the troll. Why hadn't Isla run, they wondered, why didn't she drink the flying potion and get off the bridge? What on Atalan was she doing?!

Isla was still stood there with her arm extended out in front of her. She was trying her hardest not to show fear, which was difficult when confronted by a giant troll. Her legs were still shaking uncontrollably, and it was taking all her concentration and determination to stop her arm from doing the same, but still she stood there staring at the troll with a big smile on her face.

For a few seconds, the troll didn't move. It just stared back at Isla, and then it smiled. A huge grin spread across its face, its already big brown eyes becoming even bigger.

"Hi, my name is Fizzbit, pleased to meet you, Isla." The voice that came out of the troll was not what Isla expected at all. It wasn't loud or booming but soft and gentle.

And with that, the troll started to walk across the bridge towards Isla. It moved gracefully like a cat, not a single creak or groan from the wooden planks as its bare feet lightly walked over them. The bridge didn't shudder or sway or suddenly collapse under its weight and send the pair of them plummeting to the water below.

133

As the troll walked, its huge arms hung by the side of its body as if it was carrying two giant invisible rolls of carpet. The last couple of buttons on its shirt struggled to hold its giant torso in and looked like they would pop open at any second. As it got closer to Isla, she could feel her heart racing. It felt like it was trying to get out of her chest so it could race back to the safety of the riverbank and leave its body behind.

The troll stopped a few metres in front of Isla. It towered above her, and Isla's head was about the height of its kneecaps. It held its arm out and slowly extended its little finger which was the size of a large sausage! Isla gently grabbed the troll's finger and gave it a little shake.

"Pleased to meet you, Fizzbit," Isla said, trying her hardest to disguise the shaking of her voice. She knew that at any second if the troll wanted to, it could easily toss her off the bridge and into the darkness below or simply gobble her up. But it did neither.

"So, Isla, what brings you onto this bridge?" asked Fizzbit.

"My friends and I are trying to get across to the Goblin Kingdom." As Isla answered, she turned and pointed towards Oliver and Fartybubble, except they weren't there!

"What friends?" asked Fizzbit as he scratched his mop of black hair and scanned the riverbank looking for Isla's friends.

Isla called to the pair of Unkerdunkies, and their heads popped up as they appeared from their hiding places. They both gave a sheepish wave.

"Are they shy?" asked Fizzbit as he waved back.

"I think they are just a little scared. Their elders tell them stories of a troll who lives under the bridge who throws anyone who tries to cross it into the river."

"Are you not scared?" asked Fizzbit, looking down towards Isla.

"No," lied Isla, "I told them it was just a story and they have nothing to worry about. And they haven't...have they?" asked Isla nervously.

"I'm not going to hurt you or your friends. It's just a made up story told to scare people. I've never thrown anyone into the river. It's just fake news. I've lived under this bridge all my life, and it gets lonely at times. So, anytime someone crosses it, I jump up to say hello, but as soon as they see me, they get scared and run off. Then the stories get exaggerated, and before you know it, I'm known as the troll that throws people into rivers and no one wants to cross the bridge anymore," as Fizzbit spoke his smile disappeared and a look of sadness spread across his face.

"Are there no other trolls that live with you under the bridge? What about family or friends?" asked Isla.

"I have no one. My mother and father died when I was young and ever since then I've been on my own living under this bridge," as Fizzbit spoke a single tear rolled down his cheek and dropped onto the bridge, landing with a loud plop.

"I'm so sorry to hear that," said Isla, and she gave Fizzbit's finger a little squeeze.

The troll wiped his eyes and smiled at Isla.

"Thank you," said Fizzbit.

Isla noticed her legs had stopped shaking and her heartbeat had returned to normal; she wasn't afraid anymore. Stood in front of her wasn't a vicious troll that wanted to throw her and her friends into the river, instead here was a troll that was lonely and just wanted someone to talk to.

"So, why are you going to Goblin Kingdom?" Fizzbit asked Isla.

Isla told Fizzbit about what had happened to her, about finding the book at her grandma's and ending up here on Atalan. Then meeting the Unkerdunkies and being taken to see the wizard and now the quest to find the ingredients needed for a teleportation spell that would hopefully take her home.

Fizzbit listened intently to Isla's story. He hadn't spoken to anyone for years and now the first person he did speak to was from another planet! When Isla had finished her story, Fizzbit remained silent for a few moments as he tried to take in everything she had said.

136

"Wow, you have had some day," said Fizzbit, taken aback by what he had just been told.

Isla nodded in agreement.

"And the last thing you need is a bottle of goblins' brew?" said Fizzbit

"Yes, that's it. We just need to get one bottle and then get back to Wally's house so he can create the potion and do the spell, and I can hopefully get back to my family," said Isla.

"Well, you need to be very careful, those goblins can be nasty little things. They sometimes come down to the riverbank after they've been drinking their brew all day. They get brave so they come down here shouting things at me, trying to get me to react. When I appear, they throw sticks and empty bottles at me and then run off. I tell you if they ever tried to cross my bridge, I would happily throw them into the river," said Fizzbit, getting angrier by the second.

"We will be careful. And anyway, we have our potions from the wizard. Hopefully, we can get in and out without being seen," said Isla.

"Well, that sounds a good plan to me. Right then, if you want to tell your friends they can come across, and then you can carry on with your quest. Tell them to come across once we are off the bridge and to come over one at a time. I'm not sure how much weight this old bridge can take," said Fizzbit before turning and walking back towards the riverbank, leaving a confused Isla behind. How could this bridge support the weight of a giant troll and yet struggle with a couple of tiny Unkerdunkies, she thought? Anyway, she didn't have time to try and figure that conundrum out. She had a bottle of goblin brew to find and a home to get back to.

Chapter 8

Once Oliver and Fartybubble were safely across the bridge, Isla explained to her companions that they had nothing to be scared of, that the story of the vicious troll was completely made up, and that he would never throw anyone into the river, unless of course you were a goblin.

Fartybubble looked mightily relieved by this and thanked Fizzbit for allowing them safely across the bridge so that they could continue on their quest. Oliver gave him a fist bump and told him that if he was ever passing through Forest Glades, he should pop in and say hello. Isla threw her arms around one of his enormous thighs and gave Fizzbit a hug; as she did so, he bent down and gently scooped her up with one of his giant arms and lifted her up so that she was level with his face.

"Thank you, Isla, for not running away and staying to talk to me," he said with a big beaming smile on his face.

"You're welcome," said Isla as she threw her arms around his thick neck and gave him a proper hug.

Once all the goodbyes had been said, the three adventurers set off on their way, following the map as it led them away from the bridge and towards the Goblin Kingdom, leaving Fizzbit behind them.

As they moved, the ground began to gradually climb. It wasn't very noticeable at first, but soon they found themselves on high ground. The surroundings on this side of the river were much the same as they had been on the opposite side. It was still raining hard and a heavy mist remained in the air. Isla had almost forgotten how cold and wet she was after the excitement of the bridge crossing.

As they moved forwards, they heard and saw the occasional daggermoth but nowhere near the amount they had seen on the other side of the river. Maybe the daggermoths were smart enough to stay on the opposite side to prevent themselves from becoming a culinary treat for the goblins. Either that or the goblins were good at catching them which is why there were only a few now flying around.

The trio kept pushing forward, and the path they were following kept climbing higher and higher until the uncrossable bridge was just a tiny speck in the distance far below them. As they continued forward, Isla could start to make out something through the mist. It looked to be some kind of building high above them, but with the heavy rain beating down and the thick mist all around, it was difficult to tell exactly what is was.

"What's that further up?" Isla asked, pointing up towards the structure she could vaguely see.

"That must be Goblin Kingdom," said Oliver, pointing at the map. The red arrow was pointing directly towards this mysterious building that was high above them.

"We are not far away now. It might be wise to get the invisibility potion out of the bag and have it at the ready. We need to move carefully now as there might be goblins around," said Oliver.

Isla peeled the bag out from underneath her soaking sweatshirt and pulled out the container of invisibility potion. She stashed the bag back under her top and held the bottle in her right hand.

"Shall we drink it now?" asked a nervous Fartybubble.

"No, we haven't even seen any goblins around yet," quickly answered his brother.

Oliver continued forward, leading the way. He moved slowly trying not to make any sound, continually scanning the area in search for any goblins. As they got closer towards the object, it became clearer to see exactly what is was.

It was a huge building perched high above them that resembled a castle. At the front was what looked like a large goblin's head carved out of stone. Its mouth was wide open and that seemed to be the entrance to the kingdom. Either side of this giant head were stone walls complete with battlements and a large turret at each end. On top of the turrets was a large flagpole with a flag flying from each one.

The way up to the kingdom appeared to be via concrete steps that were cut into the side of the

141

hill. Either side of the steps was a low wall and dotted along the wall every few metres or so were wooden torches burning brightly and helping to illuminate the path.

"That must be the way up," said Oliver, pointing towards the concrete steps.

Fartybubble stared up towards the kingdom above, his eyes fixated on the skull.

"It doesn't look very inviting," he said.

"Let's just get to the top of these steps and see what's up there. We have the potion on hand if we need it," Oliver said, looking over to Isla to make sure she still had the bottle in her grasp.

She nodded and held up the invisibility potion for them both to see.

"Ok, then follow me. Just keep your eyes peeled for any signs of goblins," said Oliver as he slowly started to climb the stairs. He moved carefully, taking one step at a time and constantly scanning the surrounding area. The rain was still beating down, and the heavy mist remained in the air making visibility poor. At least it would make it hard for the goblins to spot them, thought Isla, although it would also make it difficult for them to spot any goblins who were coming down the steps or who were on lookout and patrolling the battlements.

The steps seemed to go on forever, and the kingdom looked to be so high up that it was actually in the clouds. After climbing for what seemed like forever, they were still only halfway up when suddenly Oliver stopped and dropped down onto one knee. He held up a hand to indicate the others should halt.

"What is it?" whispered Fartybubble.

"Look there," said Oliver, pointing over to the hill on their right-hand side.

Isla and Fartybubble turned their heads to follow the direction in which Oliver was pointing. There lying on the hillside was a group of goblins, maybe eight or ten of them, Isla thought.

They looked just how she had imagined them to look, quite small in height and green. They had pointy ears and no hair and were all wearing the same outfit: a brown leather-looking tunic that came down just above their knees. They were barefoot, although some of them had what looked like bandages wrapped around their ankles. Scattered all around them were bottles of what Isla guessed and hoped was goblin brew as well as an assortment of what appeared to be weapons.

"Looks like they've had too much goblin brew," said Oliver with a smile, "we won't even have to set foot into the kingdom. You two wait here while I creep across and grab a bottle."

"Do you want this?" asked Isla holding up the invisibility potion.

"No need, they won't be waking up for a while," said Oliver with a chuckle.

He was right. All the goblins were sound asleep and snoring very loudly. It sounded like a load of pneumatic drills going off, and it was so loud you could hear it over the driving rain.

"Be careful," whispered Fartybubble.

Oliver carefully stepped over the low wall at the side of the steps and onto the grass. He moved with caution. The hill was steep, and the grass was wet and slippery underfoot. One false move, and he could easily slide all the way back down to the bottom.

He reached the sleeping goblins without incident and very carefully picked up the nearest bottle to him, but within seconds, he had placed it back down and moved onto another one.

"What's he doing? Why doesn't he just grab one and go?" whispered Fartybubble who was obviously starting to panic.

"He needs a full bottle," answered Isla.

She watched Oliver pick up and put down another ten bottles, each one appearing to be empty. She was willing him to find an unopened bottle so that they could make their escape without having to step foot inside the kingdom.

Oliver picked up yet another bottle, and as he did so, one of the goblins coughed and rolled onto its side and in doing so, rolled onto Oliver's foot. Oliver froze and looked down at the goblin. He was still fast asleep and once again snoring loudly.

"I can't watch," said Fartybubble, putting his head into his hands.

Isla looked on and held her breath. Oliver very carefully slid his foot from underneath the goblin's prone body without waking him. He gave a little sigh of relief followed by a thumbs up to Isla before he continued checking the remaining discarded bottles that littered the hillside.

"He's fine," whispered Isla to Fartybubble.

After checking what seemed like hundreds of bottles, Oliver carefully made his way back across the hill and re-joined the others on the steps.

"All empty, I'm afraid, these Goblins certainly like a drink," he said with a laugh.

"Now what?" asked Fartybubble, fearing what the answer was going to be.

"We keep going up the steps to the kingdom. We are bound to find a full bottle of brew up there," said Oliver, much to his brother's disappointment.

The trio set off again with Oliver leading the way. They covered the second half of the steps without any more sightings of goblins, sleeping or otherwise.

As they reached the last few steps, Oliver again stopped and dropped down onto a knee and signalled the others to do the same. The giant goblin's head was now almost directly in front of them. The only thing between them and the entrance was a path made up of tiny stones that ran the entire length of the kingdom's walls. It was

145

maybe ten metres in width, and they would have to cross this to make it inside.

From their position at the top of the steps, they could see the entire kingdom. Its battlements ran all the way around forming a square-shaped structure. There was a turret on each of its four corners, and the same flag was flying from each one.

The flag was bright red with a picture of a goblin in the middle holding a massive sword and looking like it was ready to attack.

Coming from inside the kingdom's walls, they could hear plenty of noise. It sounded like a party was in full swing. There was laughing and shouting and something that sounded like drums being played, although very badly, thought Isla.

"Right, this is the plan. There is no point us all drinking the invisibility potion and going inside the kingdom; otherwise, we won't be able to see each other. So, I will drink it and then sneak in and grab a full bottle while you two wait here. You keep hold of the potion so that if any goblins come out of the kingdom, you can turn invisible as well," said Oliver.

Fartybubble nodded in agreement. The fact he didn't have to set foot inside a place that was full of goblins sounded perfect to him.

"No, I want to go," said Isla.

Fartybubble gave her a look that suggested he thought she was crazy wanting to go.

146

"You two have helped me so much already, but I'm the one who needs the brew to help get back home. I should be the one to go and get it. You two have risked so much already for me today. Plus, you're Unkerdunkies, and the goblins don't like you. If the potion wears off while you are inside the kingdom, then what? It will be safer for me to go."

"But..." Oliver tried to argue, but Isla cut him off.

"No buts, I've made my mind up. You two stay here and keep a lookout," Isla said forcefully.

She undid the top of the potion bottle and held it up to her mouth.

"Let's see how good a wizard Wally is," she said.

They had been carrying these potions around waiting for the right time to use them, but they had no idea if they actually worked or not. The clear liquid contained in the bottle might be nothing more than water for all Isla knew. She placed the bottle to her mouth and took two big gulps of the liquid just as Wally had recommended.

The liquid may have looked like water, but it certainly didn't taste like it; in fact, it reminded Isla of the foul tasting pink drink she was always given by the dentist at the end of a scrape and polish to help rinse her mouth out. She hated the stuff and was glad that she only had to rinse with it and not swallow it.

147

This, on the other hand, she had no choice but to swallow. She forced it down, screwing up her face as she did. For one second, she thought the foul tasting potion was going to come straight back up, but luckily, she was able to keep it down.

"Is anything happening?" she asked the boys.

They both shook their heads. A couple more seconds passed and still nothing. It seemed that their plan wasn't going to happen after all. Isla stood, still staring at the boys. She felt perfectly normal and couldn't feel anything happening. The only sign she had drunk the potion was the bitter aftertaste it had left.

Just as Isla was about to give up hope that the potion was going to work, Fartybubble let out a loud gasp and pointed towards her legs.

"Look! Your legs are disappearing!"

"Really?" asked Isla. She didn't feel any different, and she could still see her legs.

"Yes, and now your body is vanishing!" cried Oliver.

The Unkerdunkies watched in amazement as Isla disappeared in front of them. Soon only her head was visible.

"And now your head has gone. You are completely invisible," said Oliver with a big grin on his face.

"So, you can't see me at all?" asked Isla, she wanted to be sure before she stepped into a kingdom full of goblins.

"The only thing we can see is the potion bottle you are holding," said Oliver. He reached over and took the bottle that was seemingly floating in mid-air.

"When you find the goblin brew, make sure you stash it in the bag under your sweatshirt. That way the goblins won't see it. If you walk out of there with it in your hand, it will look like the bottle is floating and who knows how the goblins will react to that," warned Oliver.

Isla nodded in agreement and then realised it was pointless since they couldn't see her.

"Ok," she said.

"Right, be quick as we don't know how long this potion will last for," said Oliver.

"And don't forget what Wally said. When you feel your cheeks starting to tingle, the potion is about to wear off," added Fartybubble.

"Right, got it. I'm going. I will see you soon," said Isla.

"Or not," chuckled Oliver.

Isla made her way across the path towards the entrance to the kingdom. She waved goodbye to her friends as she went and immediately realised that again it was pointless. As she walked, she could hear the stones underneath her feet crunching with every step. She tried to move as quietly as possible but then thought if she couldn't be seen then was there any point.

Instead, she raced across the path over to the wall on the left hand side of the goblin's head. She carefully peered her head around the corner and took her first look inside the kingdom.

Inside was a huge courtyard that was filled with activity. There were goblins everywhere. Dancing, drinking, shouting and banging drum-like objects with long sticks that was creating the terrible noise they had heard from outside. In the centre of the courtyard was a fire pit which had a large black pot suspended just above it by a wooden frame, which looked like it was full of boiling water. Along the left wall ran a long table that was filled with plates of food and large jugs of liquid. Some of the jugs had what Isla guessed to be water in, and some of them were filled with a murky brown liquid that could possibly be the famous brew.

Hanging down from the battlements were large ornate drapes that reached almost down to the courtyard floor. Like the flags, they were bright red in colour and covered in gold lettering and symbols. Isla didn't have a clue what they said as the lettering wasn't English or any other language she recognised.

Isla took a deep breath and then stepped through the goblin's head and into the lively courtyard. She paused for a second and waited to see if there was any reaction but thankfully nothing

150

happened. The goblins didn't react in the slightest; the potion was still working.

She quickly scanned the scene in front of her trying to locate a full bottle of goblin brew. There were plenty of empty discarded bottles lying on the floor next to an array of what Isla could only presume to be weapons.

Some of these weapons were nothing more than sticks that had been sharpened at one end to a vicious looking point. Some of the other sticks that were lying on the cobbled stone of the courtyard looked even more ferocious. One of them reminded Isla of the plastic windmills she would have at the beach to stick on top of her sandcastles except this one was much larger and was made of metal with jagged edges and had razor-sharp points. Another stick had a metal half-moon shape attached to one end that looked like it could do some serious damage. Isla certainly didn't want to get on the receiving end of any of these.

Every goblin she could see had at least one bottle in their hands, but most of them looked to be only partially full if not completely empty. By the way the goblins were flinging their arms around while they danced, a lot of the liquid was being spilt onto the floor. Isla decided to head towards the food table to see if there were any bottles on there. She really needed an unopened one so she could safely stash it in her bag. The last thing she needed was to get one that wasn't sealed properly and to get back to Wally's house and find the contents had spilt out all inside her bag.

As she moved across the courtyard towards the table, she made sure not to bump into any of the goblins or stand on their toes, as well as trying not to slip on the brew-soaked floor. She may have been invisible, but she couldn't walk through people, and she didn't want to raise any suspicions that someone was inside the kingdom. She had to be nimble on her feet to dodge some of the goblins who were dancing very energetically and throwing themselves around.

She reached the table and started to scan the contents. It was full of large silver platters of meat of some sort, bowls of red and yellow berries, and plates of who knows what. It looked like mushed up potato with bits of carrot in it; whatever it was it didn't look very appetising. Many of the jugs of the murky brown liquid were now almost empty, but the ones with what looked like water in them were almost untouched.

A couple of goblins had climbed up onto the table. One of them had picked up a large silver platter and was literally shovelling the entire contents of it into its mouth.

The other goblin was drinking a full jug of the brown stuff, and much of the liquid was missing his mouth and going all down his neck onto his leather tunic and splashing onto the table. Isla watched on as the goblin finished the entire jug before he placed it upside down on his head and let out an almighty burp.

Some of the goblins who were dancing nearby let out a loud cheer to show their appreciation of what he had done. Next second, the goblin's legs gave way from underneath him, and he fell off the table and landed in a heap on the floor, smashing the jug in the process. The cheers quickly became laughter before the dancing continued, and the goblin was left to sleep off the effects of a full jug of brew on the cobbled floor.

Isla couldn't see an unopened bottle of brew anywhere, and she was starting to panic. She didn't know how much longer she had before the potion wore off and she would be visible to an entire army of drunken goblins.

Just then, she spotted one walking towards her. It was carrying a bottle that still had its lid on, a yet to be opened bottle of goblin brew. She needed to find a way of getting it before the goblin opened it and drank the contents. The goblin was heading towards the far end of the table where there was a large glass bowl filled with something resembling trifle.

Of all the things that was on the table, this looked surprisingly appetising, and Isla started to feel hungry. She hadn't eaten anything for ages except for a couple of frothing berries, and now she could feel her stomach rumbling. She needed to take her mind off food and stay focused on the task at hand, and she needed to think fast as the goblin was about to walk past her. She stuck her leg out and tripped the goblin up. It wasn't anything clever, but it was certainly effective, but maybe too effective, as the Goblin went flying and so did the bottle.

Isla let out a gasp as the bottle flew through the air before hitting the stone cobbles. Please don't shatter, she hoped. Luckily, the bottle hit the floor with a clink and then rolled safely across the ground before coming to a rest under the table.

The goblin jumped up and looked around to see who had tripped him up. He stared straight at Isla. She froze. Surely she was still invisible because she hadn't felt her cheeks tingling yet. The Goblin marched purposefully towards her and continued straight past over to one of the goblins who was dancing nearby. A shouting match commenced followed by shoving which quickly escalated into wrestling as they both tumbled to the ground in a flurry of arms and legs.

A large group of goblins surrounded them, cheering and shouting possible encouragement, although Isla didn't understand a word they were shouting. The occasional word sounded like "fight," but that was about all she could make out. Not that it mattered, it was all the distraction she needed so that she could retrieve the bottle from under the table and stash it safely into the bag that was still under her sweatshirt without any of the goblins noticing a bottle mysteriously moving by itself.

She now had everything she needed for the teleportation spell. It was time to get out of Goblin Kingdom and back to Oliver and Fartybubble. As she headed towards the way out, past the pair of still brawling goblins on the floor, she started to feel a strange sensation in her face. A slight tingling of her cheeks. Oh no, the potion was wearing off, she thought to herself. She headed towards the doorway as quickly as she could. Her eyes were fixed on the exit through the giant goblin's head. Suddenly, her path was blocked by a group of goblins. They were screaming and shouting and pointing down towards the ground. They were pointing at her legs, thought Isla, who was really starting to panic as she started to become visible.

She quickly side-stepped to her left and ran across the centre of the courtyard past the pot of boiling water, dodging dancing goblins who were still oblivious to what was going on. She cut back towards the entrance, but another goblin blocked her way. Isla frantically looked around trying to find another way out of the kingdom since her path to the main entrance was well and truly blocked. She spotted a couple of wooden doors that seemed to lead up to the battlements, but they were surrounded by goblins and appeared locked anyway.

More and more goblins were now pointing towards her and not just at her legs. They were staring straight at her. She watched in horror as many of the goblins started to retrieve their weapons from the floor and begin waving them around menacingly. She was now completely surrounded and had nowhere left to run. Maybe she could try introducing herself like she had done with Fizzbit, but by the looks of the angry faces staring back at her, she decided that tactic wouldn't work here.

She had come so far in her quest to get back home and had failed at the final hurdle. She felt sick in her stomach, although that could have been the hunger. She was trapped inside the kingdom surrounded by a horde of drunken, angry, and armed goblins, and she didn't have her friends this time to help her. She felt scared and alone.

"Hey, goblins, I thought you were tough, but I bet I could kick each one of your butts!"

The goblins all turned around to face the entrance where the voice had come from. Stood under the giant goblin's head was Oliver or at least part of him as his legs were missing.

Isla watched on in amazement as her friend disappeared right in front of her eyes. He must have drunk the potion, she thought. The sight of a disappearing Unkerdunkie in their kingdom sent the goblins crazy. They were shouting at each other, scratching their heads, and looking behind the drapes to try and find him. The distraction meant that the goblins' attention had been taken off Isla for a few seconds, and it might be all the time she needed to escape.

Isla headed towards the entrance. Many of the goblins now had their backs to her or were too busy trying to find the vanishing Unkerdunkie, and she hoped she could slip out without them noticing. She had only taken a couple of steps when a pointy stick appeared in front of her blocking the way. The goblin who was holding it was screaming something at her. Isla held up her hands to show that she wasn't a threat and retreated back towards the centre of the courtyard.

"Where are you, Oliver? I really need some help," she whispered.

Suddenly, there was a loud crash from behind her that made her jump. She spun round to see that the pot of boiling water had been knocked over. As the water hit the cobbled floor, a huge cloud of steam rose into the air. Isla watched on as one of the sticks from the wooden frame that had held the pot in position appeared to float. This must have been Oliver's doing, she thought to herself, but just what was he up to?

The end of the stick was placed into the fire pit, and within seconds it was burning brightly. A few of the goblins approached the pit, but the sight of a flaming stick mysteriously floating through the air had them quickly retreating. The stick was being wafted around to keep the goblins at bay as it moved across the courtyard towards one of the drapes that was hanging down near the large table.

"Good idea," Isla said to herself as she started to realise what Oliver was doing.

She watched as the burning stick came into contact with the drape and a moment later WHOOSH. Whatever material the drapes were made from, they were highly flammable as the fire took hold in seconds. The flames quickly spread up the drape towards the battlements creating thick black plumes of smoke that started to fill the courtyard and create chaos inside. Goblins were running all over the place, some of them ran towards the table in an attempt to grab the water jugs to try and fight the fire, but as they got close, they were pelted with food. Meat was being skimmed across the courtyard as if they were frisbees; berries were flung at the approaching goblins like pellets from a catapult.

Whole plates of the mashed potato carrot mix were being launched into the air followed by spoonfuls of the trifle type dessert. It was as if a one-sided food fight had erupted inside the kingdom, and the goblins had no idea who was causing it. There was now complete pandemonium within the courtyard as goblins were slipping and sliding on the food and falling flat on their faces; although, some of them appeared to be falling over due to the large amounts of brew they had drunk!

Others were trying desperately to put out the now raging inferno while some were swinging their weapons into thin air in a vain attempt to strike an invisible Unkerdunkie. As Isla watched the scene unfold in front of her, she felt something grab her right arm. She let out a gasp and turned to see what it was, expecting to be confronted by an angry goblin, but to her surprise and relief, nobody was there.

"It's time to go," came a voice, seemingly from nowhere. It was Oliver.

Before Isla had chance to say anything, she felt a tug at her arm as Oliver pulled her towards the entrance. The goblins were now well and truly distracted, and their path out of the kingdom was clear. As she ran, Isla looked to her right and saw Oliver's feet.

"The potion's wearing off," she cried.

"I know, I can feel my cheeks tingling. We need to get out of here fast," replied Oliver.

The pair raced out through the stone goblin's open mouth and back onto the path outside leaving the madness behind. By this time, Oliver was back to being completely visible.

"Where's Fartybubble?" shouted Isla.

"He's there," Oliver replied, pointing towards the steps.

Isla looked over and spotted him. He was a couple of steps from the top and crouched down so that he couldn't be seen from the kingdom.

"Did you get a bottle of brew?" Oliver asked Isla.

"Yes," she replied, tapping the bag under her sweatshirt.

"Then let's go," said Oliver as he pulled Isla by the arm towards the steps.

The three of them started to race down the steps as quickly as they could, but they hadn't got far when they came to a halt. Coming up towards them was the group of goblins they had passed earlier, although now they were wide awake and looking angry. Maybe all the commotion from the kingdom had woken them, and possibly the sight of black smoke billowing out above the battlements was what had made them angry. Whatever it was, they were heading up the steps and straight towards them with their weapons drawn.

"Change of plan, we need to find another way down," shouted Oliver as he shepherded Isla and Fartybubble back up the steps and towards the kingdom.

When they reached the top, they took a left and raced along the stone path. They could hear the shouting and screaming from within the kingdom as the goblins fought to put out the fire. Oliver reached the end of the path first and followed it around to the right. It seemed to go around the entire perimeter of the kingdom.

"Come on, hurry up," he shouted back to the others who followed behind.

As he ran along the path, he looked over to his left to see if there was any way down to safety from this side of the kingdom. There were no steps cut into the hill on this side, and whereas the hill at the front was fairly steep, on this side it was more of a vertical drop straight down to the ground far below.

"Is this a good time to suggest using the flying potion?" panted Fartybubble as he struggled to keep up with Oliver and Isla.

"Yes, bro, I think this is the perfect time," shouted Oliver as he stopped running and turned to Isla, "Quickly, get the potion out of the bag."

Isla pulled the bag out from under her sweatshirt and delved inside desperately trying to find the tiny container of flying potion. It wasn't easy since the bottle was so small and the bag was full of all the things they had collected on their quest, plus Isla's hands were shaking uncontrollably.

As she searched the bag, the sounds of feet crunching across the stones grew louder and louder as the goblins got closer.

"Hurry," urged Oliver.

"Goblins," screamed Fartybubble.

The pursuing horde came flying around the corner and were closing in fast.

"I've found it," shouted Isla as she pulled the tiny bottle from out the canvas bag and held it up.

161

Oliver grabbed it off her and quickly undid the lid.

"Tiny sip each, remember," he shouted as he took a small swig of the potion.

He passed the bottle to Isla who did the same and then finally Fartybubble who poured the remaining liquid down his throat as quickly as possible. Oliver stepped forward to the edge of the drop and looked down. Isla joined him to his right while Fartybubble was on his left looking back towards the onrushing goblins. As Isla reached the edge of the drop, she felt her legs go funny. Wow, that was a really long way down, she thought.

"How do we know if the potion has worked?" asked Isla.

"Only one way to find out," replied Oliver.

He grabbed Isla and Fartybubble by their hands and jumped.

Chapter 9

As soon as they jumped, Isla felt her stomach lurch and churn. It felt the same as when her dad went over a bump in the road slightly too fast, or the ride at the theme park that took you straight up into the air and then dropped you, so you fell back towards the ground at frightening speed. Only this time she wasn't falling.

"I'M FLYING," screamed Isla with pure excitement.

She wasn't plummeting uncontrollably towards the ground below, instead she was soaring through the sky with the wind in her face. This was amazing, she thought as she looked over to her right to see where Oliver and Fartybubble were. Oliver had his arms and legs spread out in a star shape and was laughing and shouting. He was obviously enjoying the experience. Fartybubble, on the other hand, not so much. He had his usual look of fear across his face that had been there for the majority of the journey.

"How do you steer?!" he shouted.

Isla scanned the landscape, doing her best to get her bearings. She knew the kingdom was directly behind her so the river and the bridge must be somewhere over to the left.

"Let's head towards the bridge," Isla shouted over to Oliver as loudly as she could so to be heard over the wind. Oliver nodded and gave a thumbs up.

"Now, how do you steer?" Isla said mainly to herself.

She rolled her body to the left and dropped her left shoulder towards the ground. Immediately she changed direction and was now facing back towards the river. The kingdom was now on her left side; she could still see clouds of smoke billowing out over the battlements although not as much as before. Maybe the goblins had managed to get the fire under control. Isla rolled again slightly to the left and flew over the top of the steps. Looking down, she could see the group of goblins who had been chasing them were now descending the steps.

It looked like they had been joined by another group who had come out of the kingdom and had also taken up the chase. They are not giving up easily, thought Isla, and she knew she and her friends weren't out of danger just yet. If they could make it to the bridge and back across to the other side of the river, then they would be safe, at least from the goblins. There was no way they would follow them across the bridge knowing that a huge scary troll lived under there who they often liked to tease and throw things at.

As Isla scanned ahead, she spotted the bridge in the distance; she was heading pretty much straight for it. She glanced over her shoulder and saw that Oliver and Fartybubble were right behind. Isla extended her right arm and gave it her best Superman impression. As she flew through the air, she tried to take it all in. It was amazing to think that she was actually flying. She had to say it out loud a few times almost as a way to convince herself it was actually happening.

"I'm flying, this is amazing, I am actually fly…. FALLING!" the words tumbled out of her mouth as she started to drop out of the sky.

Wally had warned them that the potion wouldn't last long, and he wasn't wrong. Isla had been flying for less than 30 seconds. She tried waving her arms around and frantically kicking her legs, but nothing was slowing her descent. She looked down towards the ground that was quickly approaching. The river was still a little way away, and she was heading straight for the hard ground.

Isla pulled her knees up into her chest and adopted a brace position, similar to what they always showed you on an airplane before any flight. She was about to have a crash landing of her own so thought the brace position seemed appropriate. She closed her eyes and prepared for impact.

She hit the ground bottom first with a splash. Where she had landed was like a bog, and the ground was completely waterlogged. She skidded along the floor for a few metres getting covered in mud and grass and getting soaked through to the skin, but luckily she was still in one piece. As she looked up from where she had come to a rest, she saw a pair of feet sliding towards her.

"Uff," came the cry from Oliver as he skidded straight into Isla.

"Oww," cried Isla.

As Oliver tried to pull himself up off the ground, he too was wiped out by Fartybubble who came flying through the mud and ended up in a big heap on top of both Oliver and Isla.

"Is everyone ok?" asked Oliver from his position in the middle of an Isla and Fartybubble sandwich.

His brother climbed off him and fell onto the floor holding his ankle. He was covered from head to toe in mud. The only part of him that was visible were his eyes and he resembled some kind of swamp monster.

"My ankle really hurts. I'm not sure I can walk on it."

Oliver pulled himself off Isla and held out his hand to help her up. She gingerly got to her feet holding her bottom.

"I think I've bruised my bum," she said, wincing.

Oliver flopped back down onto the ground, landing with a squelch, and held his left shoulder.

"Yeah, I think I've done the same to my shoulder. I landed pretty hard."

Isla looked around trying to work out exactly where they had landed and where they were in relation to the bridge. She couldn't spot the bridge but the one thing she did spot were…GOBLINS.

They had managed to get down to the bottom of the steps and had spotted where the trio had crash landed and were now approaching fast.

"We have a problem," said Isla, her voice shaking with fear.

Oliver looked up from his seated position, and Isla motioned for him to turn around. He looked over his left shoulder and saw the goblins closing in.

"We need to run," he shouted, but as soon as he stood up, he slipped on the mud and fall back onto the ground letting out a moan.

"I can't run. My ankle hurts too much," sobbed Fartybubble.

"Run, Isla, we will try and distract them. You have everything you need for the spell. Take this and go," Oliver shouted, throwing Isla the map that he had managed to keep hold of. The red arrow was now pointing back towards Wally's house.

"I'm not leaving you two here. It's over," Isla said with her head bowed. Tears started to trickle down her face as the goblins arrived.

Fartybubble dragged himself off the ground and hobbled to his feet; he raised his hands and clenched his fists.

"DO YOU KNOW WHAT KIND OF DAY WE'VE HAD?! I'VE BEEN CHASED BY BULLHOUNDS, MY BROTHER'S BEEN

ATTACKED BY A VINECATCHER, WE ALMOST GOT BURNED ALIVE BY A BUZZAGON AND NOW THIS. I'VE NOT COME ALL THIS WAY TO BE STOPPED BY A FEW GOBLINS. IF IT'S A FIGHT YOU WANT THEN IT'S A FIGHT YOU'VE GOT," Fartybubble screamed at the top of his voice.

Isla and Oliver shot each other a look of complete surprise. They never for a second thought he would react like this.

"Umm, bro, what are you doing?" whispered Oliver.

"It's ok, I've got this," replied his brother.

The goblins stood there in total disbelief. They looked at Fartybubble, then at each other and then back at Fartybubble. Then they burst out laughing and for a second, Isla thought they might let them go, but unfortunately, the laughing quickly stopped, and a look of anger appeared on their faces. With their weapons raised, they walked towards Fartybubble.

"Bro, it's not working," whispered Oliver, panic now setting in.

"I know. I'm not sure what came over me," cried Fartybubble, his fists were still raised but now visibly shaking.

The goblins took another couple of steps forward and then stopped; a look of fear spread across their faces. They lowered their weapons and started to retreat.

"It's working," gasped Oliver.

"GO ON AWAY WITH YOU AND DON'T COME BACK!" screamed Fartybubble.

The brave little Unkerdunkie puffed out his chest and let out a roar, but the sound that was heard all around was a much louder and terrifying roar that didn't come from Fartybubble. The sound came from behind Isla and almost made her jump out of her skin. She spun around to see what had made such a sound and there stood behind her looking as mean as he could was Fizzbit! The sight of the huge troll had caused the goblins to retreat, and they were now fleeing back towards the steps and the relative safety of the Goblin Kingdom.

"Fizzbit," shouted Isla as she threw her arms around him or at least partially around one of his legs.

"What are you doing here?" she asked with a big smile on her face.

"I saw smoke coming from the kingdom and thought you might be in trouble, so, I came to help," said Fizzbit in his soft and gentle voice.

"Thank you so much, you saved our lives," tears were streaming down Isla's face but instead of sadness they were tears of joy and relief.

"Did you get what you needed for your potion?" asked Fizzbit.

Isla nodded and then pulled the bag from out under her sweatshirt to check that she hadn't dropped anything and that the bottle of brew was

169

still intact after their daring escape and crash landing. She was very relieved to see everything was still safely inside the bag and that the bottle was in one piece with the lid still firmly in place. She held the bag up for everyone to see.

"Yep, we have everything we need."

Oliver slowly pulled himself off the ground. His legs were caked in mud, and he was still holding his shoulder. He looked over to his brother.

"Hey, bro, that was amazing. What you just did then was one of the bravest things I've ever seen," said Oliver with a huge smile on his face.

"Thank you," replied Fartybubble, wiping mud away from his face. "I play at being a warrior often enough and today, just for a moment, I got to be one."

Oliver nodded in agreement. "You are a warrior, bro."

"Can we go home now, though?" said Fartybubble. Through all the mud you could just about make out a huge grin on his face.

"Do you need a lift?" asked Fizzbit.

"A lift?" said Isla surprised. She wasn't really sure what sort of mode of transport a huge troll would take.

"Yes, a lift," the giant troll said with a smile.

Fizzbit bent down and picked up Isla and lifted her high above his head and onto his shoulders. He then scooped up Oliver and Fartybubble and carried them in each arm.

"Just tell me the way," Fizzbit called up to Isla who still had hold of the map. "Oh, and hold on tight!"

Chapter 10

Being carried on the shoulders of a giant troll was a much better way to travel through Atalan, Isla thought to herself as they made the journey back to Wally's. Fizzbit moved like lightning and covered the terrain with ease. Perched high up on his shoulders, Isla got to see Atalan in a whole new way. It really was a beautiful and magical place especially when you were not being chased by buzzagons or goblins or any other kind of creature.

They raced through Snowy Point with Fizzbit leaving giant footprints in the snow as he went. Isla spotted a couple of buzzagons way off in the distance flying high over the mountain tops.

They really were beautiful creatures especially from this distance, Isla thought. They moved through the sky so effortlessly for such huge animals. She managed to take her phone out and record a video of a pair of buzzagons swooping through the grey skies. Wait till she showed her friends this, she thought. It would top even the best YouTube videos of pandas sneezing and dogs farting that were usually shared between them. No one else would have seen a buzzagon, although Isla was sure her friend Kelly Green would claim that she had because according to her, she had seen and done everything.

Through Snowy Point they went, back into the sunshine and greenery of Forest Glades, past the frothing berry orchard where many of the trees were now bare after the elemamoths had feasted on the berries.

Across the rolling fields they went, through the forest until they reached the clearing where Wally's house stood. Not once had Fizzbit slowed down, and the journey back to the wizard's had taken no time at all.

"We are here," shouted Isla from her position high up.

Fizzbit came to a stop and gently put his passengers down. He looked over to the small house he could see through the trees and undergrowth.

"Is that Wally's house?" Fizzbit asked Isla. She nodded back.

"I think I will wait outside," the giant troll said with a chuckle as he looked at the size of the front door.

"Thank you so much for helping us. I really appreciate it from the bottom of my heart," said Isla as she gave her new friend one more hug.

"I hope the spell works and you get home safely to your family," said Fizzbit.

"Thank you," replied Isla. She could feel herself starting to get emotional. She was obviously excited about the prospect of going home, but she had met some wonderful people and had made some good friends, and she was going to miss them all.

"Just promise me one thing," said Fizzbit.

"Anything," replied Isla.

"If you ever come back to Atalan, make sure you come and visit me," as Fizzbit spoke, a giant tear fell from his eye and hit the ground with a loud splash.

"Of course," replied Isla as she buried her head into the giant troll's leg and gave him a big hug as tears rolled down her face.

"We should really be going," said Oliver softly. He felt bad breaking the pair up, but he and his brother needed to get back to their village, and they didn't want to leave until they had seen their quest through to the end and Isla was safely back home.

Isla peeled herself off Fizzbit and wiped her eyes. She said one last farewell while the boys each gave him a goodbye fist bump. Once that was done, Oliver walked over to the wizard's door and gave the lion's head knocker two loud bangs. After a short while, there was the usual sound of jangling keys from the other side of the door before Wally opened it. He stood in the doorway with a look of surprise on his face. Isla wasn't sure if that was due to the fact they had returned or because a huge troll was stood in the clearing towering over his magic tree.

"We've got everything you need for the spell," said Isla, holding up the bag of goodies.

"Well, in that case, you better come inside," said Wally, gesturing them in.

Isla led the way followed by Oliver and finally Fartybubble.

"Is your friend staying outside?" asked Wally, signalling towards Fizzbit.

"He's a little too big for the door," said Isla.

"Suit yourself," said Wally with a shrug as he closed the front door behind him.

Wally walked over to the large table and motioned for Isla to put the bag on there. The room looked pretty much the same as when they had left, and Wally was still dressed in the same attire. As he rummaged through the bag to make sure everything was there, he looked up at the three of them.

They were all covered in mud and had pieces of grass sticking out of their clothes. Oliver's hat was all crumpled, and Fartybubble had lost his altogether, and he still resembled a relative of the Swamp Thing. Isla's clothes had dried a little during the journey back but were still wet through and starting to smell.

"Have much trouble getting the stuff?" asked Wally.

All three looked at each other before answering Wally.

"Not at all," lied Isla.

"Piece of cake," added Oliver.

Fartybubble remained quiet, instead he just shook his head.

Wally raised an eyebrow and stroked his beard. He wasn't quite convinced by their answers.

"Well, everything is here so let's get this potion made," said Wally, grabbing the spell book labelled T that was still on the table. He turned to the teleportation spell and started to read the instructions.

First thing he did was grab an implement from the table that looked similar to a pestle and mortar. Isla recognised it as it looked almost identical to one her mum had. Wally placed the magic leaf in first and crushed it up using the pestle. He then added the frothing berries. He poured them all into the mortar before taking a handful back out. He added another couple back in before finally taking one more out.

When he seemed happy that the right amount was in, he started crushing them up, the berries all bursting under his pestle which turned the mortar a dark red colour. Once he was happy with the consistency, he took the two buzzagon feathers from out of the bag and crushed them up in his hands before carefully sprinkling them into the mixture. He gave it a little stir and then added the whiteflower seeds.

It was just like watching her mum bake a cake, thought Isla. The final ingredient needed was the goblin brew. Wally picked up the bottle and unscrewed the lid and held it up to his nose. As he sniffed the liquid inside, he pulled his head back sharply.

"This stuff stinks. I don't know how those goblins can drink so much of it," Wally said, holding his nose.

He carefully tipped the bottle up and poured some of the brew into his mixture before giving it a stir. He then repeated the process of adding some goblin brew and stirring over and over again until the bottle was almost empty.

"The potion is almost done. I now need your picture," said Wally, turning to Isla.

Isla pulled her phone from her back pocket and unlocked it. As she did, she noticed something a little bit worrying. The screen was displaying that only two percent battery was remaining. Filming the buzzagons must have drained it, and she hadn't noticed. A bit of panic started to set in that the phone might cut out before Wally had a chance to cast his spell. Isla went immediately into her pictures and found the one she was after. She handed the phone to Wally who placed it on the table with the screen facing up, the picture of Isla with her parents and Grandma displayed for everyone to see.

"Now time to cast the spell," said Wally.

He double checked his book to make sure he knew exactly what he had to say before picking up his wand from the table. He cleared his throat and adjusted his hat. All the time this was going on, Isla was willing him in her head to get on with it. Her eyes were fixed on the phone's screen as she stared intently at the battery symbol.

When Wally was finally ready, he placed the tip of his wand into the potion which had now turned a dark purple colour. As he held the wand in the liquid, something started to happen. The wand started to glow red and steam started to rise up out of the mortar. He lifted his wand and held it directly above the phone and started to read out the spell.

"Teleportation spell we are asking you, please take us off to somewhere new."

As the last word left his mouth, a small drop of potion fell from the wand and down towards the phone's screen that was still displaying the picture. Just as the liquid was about to make contact with the phone, the battery died, and the screen went blank.

Isla watched on in horror as the drop of potion plopped onto the phone and nothing happened. She could hardly believe it. After everything they had gone through to get all the ingredients for the spell and now for this to happen. To be so close to getting home only to be denied the opportunity at the very last second.

"NOOOOO," she screamed at the top of her lungs which made Oliver and Fartybubble jump.

"What happened?" asked Oliver, looking a little confused.

"The phone's run out of charge. The battery has died. I can't get home," as Isla said it, she slumped to the floor and held her head in her hands.

Oliver walked over to her and put his hand on her shoulder trying to console her.

"I'm sorry," he said, not really knowing what else to say.

No one really knew what to say and for a few moments the room was silent except for the sound of Isla's sobbing.

"LOOK!" shouted Fartybubble, making everyone jump.

Isla wiped her eyes and looked up to see what Fartybubble was shouting at. He was pointing at the table. The phone had started vibrating. It was shaking so much it was making some of the glasses and beakers on the table rattle loudly.

"It's working, the spell is working," cried Wally with a look of delight on his face.

The phone suddenly burst into life and a bright white light shot out of the screen lighting up the ceiling high above.

"Quickly, Isla, I don't know how long it will last," shouted Wally with a sense of urgency.

Isla jumped up from the floor. She turned to Oliver and wrapped her arms around him and gave him a huge hug.

"Thank you for everything. I will never forget you."

179

"Have a safe journey," replied Oliver. He was trying his hardest not to show emotion, but his eyes were starting to fill with tears.

Isla raced over to Fartybubble and gave him a big hug as well.

"And thank you as well. I couldn't have done this without you two. I will miss you."

"We will miss you too," replied Fartybubble, tears rolling down his face.

"Hurry, Isla, the spell could wear off at any second," shouted Wally.

"What do I do?" Isla asked the wizard.

"You need to pick up the phone, hold it in front of you, and walk into the light," replied Wally.

Isla grabbed the phone from off the table and lifted it up in front of her.

"Thank you, Wally, you really are a fantastic wizard."

Wally blushed slightly as he smiled and gave Isla a wink.

Isla turned to her two friends and gave them one last thumbs up before she stepped forward into the light.

Chapter 11

For a few moments, Isla couldn't see anything apart from complete whiteness all around her. She blinked her eyes a few times as she tried to adjust to the brightness. Slowly the light started to dim, and she started to make out a few shapes in the distance; one of the shapes looked very much like a tree.

For a second, her heart sank. Surely she wasn't back in the Atalan forest, she thought. Maybe the spell hadn't worked properly. Maybe the phone dying just before the spell had been cast had somehow affected it, or possibly the fact they used a picture from a phone instead of a book had caused it to go wrong.

Nervously, Isla stepped forwards out of the light into bright sunshine and onto freshly mowed grass. She hardly dared look up to see what was in front of her. Directly opposite her was indeed a tree. It was a willow tree and it belonged to her grandma. She was finally home.

Isla punched the air in delight and let out a cry of pure happiness. She could hardly believe she was back and that the spell had actually worked. She looked down and gave herself a quick check over to make sure nothing crazy had happened during teleportation. She was relieved to see that nothing had. She was also happy to see that she still had hold of her phone. As well as that, her clothes had returned to normal and were in the same state as when she had first arrived at Grandma's. They were no longer soaking wet or caked in mud with pieces of grass sticking out from all over the place.

After checking herself, Isla then checked the driveway. She was expecting to see her parents' car there. She didn't know how long she had been away, but it must have been a few days at least. She knew her grandma was getting on a bit, but she would definitely notice Isla was missing and report it to her parents, and they would surely race round as soon as possible. But there was no sign of her parents' car or any police cars or other vehicles for that matter. Everything looked the same as when she had arrived, on the outside at least.

Isla walked over the garden to the front door. She went to knock but decided instead to try the handle. She gave it a gentle turn, and the door opened with the usual creek. Isla stepped inside the hallway and noticed the pendulum clock was showing half past one. It wasn't much later than when she was last at Grandma's. Although, of course, she didn't know how many days later it was.

As Isla stood in the hallway, she could hear a noise coming from the kitchen. She walked into the lounge and spotted the box of bric-a-brac was still on the table. Grandma obviously hadn't got around to moving it yet. Isla walked through the lounge and into the kitchen, and there stood at the sink washing the pots was her grandma.

182

"Oh, hello dear, have you looked through those boxes already? That didn't take you long," said Grandma, looking up from the dishes. She wasn't shocked or surprised to see Isla in the slightest.

"How long have I been?" asked Isla, a little confused. This wasn't really the reaction she had been expecting.

"Only a few minutes," answered her grandma.

"Oh," said Isla who was now totally confused

"Did you not find anything of interest in the boxes?" asked Grandma.

"Umm, well, I wouldn't say nothing of interest," said Isla.

"Well, would you like a hot chocolate? I was just about to make myself one," said Grandma.

Isla nodded before racing over to her Grandma and wrapping her arms tightly around her.

"I love you, Grandma."

"Oh dear, I love you too," answered Grandma as she hugged Isla back.

"Could I ring Mum and Dad please, Grandma?" asked Isla.

"Already? But they've not long left," answered Grandma.

"I know," said Isla, "I just miss them."

Printed in Great Britain
by Amazon